THE RED CARPET

THE DIAL PRESS

THE RED CARPET

Bangalore Stories

Lavanya Sankaran

The Dial Press

THE RED CARPET
BANGALORE STORIES
A Dial Press Book / May 2005

Published by The Dial Press
A Division of Random House, Inc.
New York, New York

The story "The Red Carpet" appeared in the December 2003 issue of
the *Atlantic Monthly*.

Book design by Lynn Newmark

The Dial Press is a registered trademark of Random House, Inc., and the
colophon is a trademark of Random House, Inc.

Library of Congress Cataloging-in-Publication Data
Sankaran, Lavanya.
The red carpet : Bangalore stories / Lavanya Sankaran.
p. cm.
ISBN: 0-385-33817-1
1. Conflict of generations—Fiction.
2. Bangalore (India)—Fiction.
PR9499.4.S26 R43 2005
823'.92 22   2004060918

Printed in the United States of America
Published simultaneously in Canada

www.dialpress.com

10   9   8   7   6   5   4   3   2   1
BVG

for my husband, Nikhil Kumar,
and
for my parents, Laxam Sankaran and S. Sankaran

past perfect, present perfect

CONTENTS

BOMBAY
THIS

Ramu studied the animated woman in front of him, a slight smile on his lips. And apart from the minor variances: his gender, darker skin color, the carefully trimmed goatee resting on his chin, and the worrisome hairline that danced away from his forehead in the coy manner that plagued so many men in their early thirties, it was practically a Mona Lisa smile—full of mystery and hidden amusement.

The woman, Ashwini, was a recent import to the city, having moved to Bangalore with her parents after living her whole life in Bombay. After a year here, she was still going through withdrawal symptoms, and her conversation was frequently colored with Bombay this and Bombay that and in Bombay we and o god why can't Bangalore? If she were smart, he thought, she would learn that this invariably irritated her listeners, many of whom had lived in other parts of the country and indeed the world, but on the whole had managed to assimilate into this southern city with considerably more grace. One saw her everywhere however, in all the pubs and all the parties, because in addition to her list of nostalgic complaints, she was also armed with a lot of verve and fun. She was up for anything, a good-time charlie, a bustling ball of energy and laughter, a squeal and hug and kiss for everybody, her hips grinding inadvertently but pleasantly against the men she talked to as her bottom swayed happily to passing bits of music.

When she met people at parties, she didn't (as Ramu might) smile, chat, and withdraw from them until the next party. Instead she had the knack of making friends, and (before they knew it) of climbing deep into their lives. Then, there she'd be: visiting, cooing to their children, listening with concern to tales of their mothers-in-law, proffering advice on where to get the best blouse tailor versus the best pant tailor and who caters the best party soufflés, all of which she amazingly seemed to know, pulled out of the air of a strange and new city by some inexplicable consumerist osmosis. Every party Ramu attended recently had some contribution by her: Ashwini did the decorations, the hostess would say. Ashwini brought the sweet. Do you like the curtains? Ashwini showed me where to buy them. And all this, of course, to Ashwini's tune of Bombay this and Bombay that.

As far as Ramu was concerned, she was just one of those women one met in the evenings and promptly forgot about in the mornings. It was only recently that his interest had taken a direct and more personal turn.

Now he studied her and realized how self-defeating her actions were. He felt a sudden urge to explain this to her (first, of course, sitting her down in a corner armchair, extinguishing her cigarette, placing her drink on a side table, and waiting for her eyes to focus on him instead of dancing about the room): Bangalore was a strange city, a potpourri of beggars and billionaires and determinedly laid-back ways. People dressed down here, not just on Fridays, but every day, and more so on occasions—and gently derided those who didn't. They spoke of their city's attractions to visitors in tones of disparaging surprise. Oh. You like the weather? Yeah, it's okay. I guess. Cool. Blue skies and all. Cosmopolitan people, you think? Yeah, they're a mixed bag. Different, one-*tharah* types. Not so hard-and-fast. A chill crowd, like. Doing ultra-cool things *chumma*, simply, for no reason other than to do it.

"See the software lads," he could say, by way of example. See the software lads shrug off their stock options. (No, no, I'm *still* a simple *saaru-soru* rasam-and-rice guy at heart.) See the software lads morph their inner walter mitty into alfred doolittle (I swear, da, it was just a little bit of blooming luck). See them stab each other in the back trying to prove that they too can please-kindly-adjust, the mantra that the city uses to exact merciless compromise from all of its denizens.

Such self-deprecation appeared modern, with its blue jeans and infotech ways, but was actually a very old courtesy. Deride yourself so others may praise you. Did Ashwini know this? Did she know she was spreading irritation before her like a virus? And here, Ramu found his thoughts slowing to a halt. Perhaps she wasn't. Perhaps no one else was really bothered by it. Actually, until recently, neither was he, previously just swatting her behavior out of his mind as he might a fly. At parties, after all, one met all sorts of people and thought nothing further of it.

Until recently.

"Oh god," Ashwini was saying, "you should just see them,

yaar. Everybody does it, all the time. In parties, in bars, in people's houses. You're talking to somebody, and then suddenly, they're doing a line. It's crazy!"

The people listening to the excited pitch of her voice did so with an air of fascinated disapproval, like height-of-empire englishwomen being regaled with missionary tales of naughty hindoo heathens. Ashwini was just back from a trip north, and deeply impressed by the spread of cocaine in polite Bombay society. I mean, she said, you don't see anything like that here. In Bangalore. No indeed, thought her listeners primly, all of whom smoked the occasional joint, but nothing more. They were strictly old-fashioned in that way.

"Did you try any?" someone asked.

"Oh god, no! Even though my friends—from good families, you know, from big industrial families—even though they all kept asking me to do it, I said no. They kept saying: god, you're so cool, so hip, why don't you try it? I said, nothing doing, I'll drink all the vodka and smoke as many joints as you like," said Ashwini, proceeding to demonstrate, "but this, nothing doing! Shit *yaar*, imagine me doing cocaine!"

Shit, thought Ramu, imagine anyone giving a damn.

Three days later, Ramu left his mother's presence with a vague feeling of doom.

This was not going to work.

Entrusting such a crucial mission to his mother was becoming a farce: like sending someone to the market with strict instructions to buy luscious, juicy fruit, and having them repeatedly, idiotically, come home with boring, healthy-for-you vegetables.

Yet Ramu couldn't extricate himself easily. He was, like any unmonk, a captive of his desires.

In recent months, Ramu had found himself attracted, regrettably, not to the pretty young things he met all over the place (for apart from a fierce desire to shag them, there was nothing else he could imagine doing with them); rather, he found himself being drawn to the wives in his circle of friends. Women his own age, claimed by marriage and scarred by childbirth years before; women who waded comfortably between dirty diapers and smelly spouses and stressful jobs and thieving servants and occasional bright evenings filled with beer and good cheer. They laughed easily with him, without that brittle coquetry that younger, single women offered in the name of flirting. They sometimes shone with all the gloss of a recent visit to the beauty parlor, but were more frequently without makeup, displaying casually hirsute underarms and rough-stubbled legs dressed in old shorts. Yet he was seized with feverish desires to taste the beaded sweat on their upper lips as they frowned over some chore, and to bury his nose and mouth and body in the liquid warmth between their thighs. He wanted to make homes with them. He wanted to fill himself with their comfortable, lazy sexuality. He wanted to spend hours in their kitchens cooking vast and creative Sunday meals with them, and then spend hours more eating and drinking, and lounging around with newspapers, absentmindedly rubbing toes to the distant clatter of maids cleaning up the debris in the kitchen. He wanted to father their children. He wanted to have little domestic quarrels about curtains, and long conversations about career issues, and exchange bright little secret jokes in whispers about people they both knew.

It was time to be married.

Ramu's decision to supplement his wife-finding efforts with his mother's was a purely practical one. Ma had resources he would never have access to. Ma had a lifetime membership to that hidden, systemic device, specially designed for men in his position: the matrimonial industry, a sinister social syndicate redolent with its own brokers and goons and gossip.

Ma was a blessing. Effectively disguised.

As he'd expected, she shot into action. Ma had first broached the subject of his marriage five years earlier, but had been shouted at for her pains. Mind your own business, Ramu had said. She was doing nothing else, but she didn't tell him that, instead biding her time, waiting patiently for the right psychological moment to bring to her son's disposal a vast arsenal of resources, contacts, and networking facilities. Ma was a one-woman marriage-bureau-in-waiting. Waiting, that is, to match her Long-lived *Chiranjeevi* with someone else's Very-lucky *Sowbhagyavathi*; and to print up those invitations: Chi. *Ramu, son-of-herself,* to wed Sow, *girl-from-good-family. Please do come.*

This afternoon's conversation, like so many in recent days, was littered with the fruits of her research and followed a pattern that Ramu, with veteran discomfort, was beginning to recognize: Ma, bright, cheerful, animated; himself, uneasy, like a tethered animal sensing a storm; uneasy, and wondering about the forces of nature he had inadvertently released.

"So, what do you think?" she pressed him, as she served him with crisp fried *vadas* and a cup of tea.

Ramu dragged a vada through the coconut chutney, not willing to commit himself.

"So there is this Sundaram girl," she said, repeating herself. "Very nice. Very pretty. Good choice."

Ramu couldn't sit through it all again without comment. "Pretty? Please, Ma! She has a face like a dog's behind."

"Okay. Not so pretty, then. But a very good family, nevertheless. Very well-to-do. Eat."

She eyed him with speculative hope. "Or there is that other girl, from Visakhapatnam. Excellent family, decent people, and I really like her, Ramu. What is her name? Sukanya. She reminds me of myself when I got married. . . ."

Ramu's father grunted, in the wary manner of a man reminded of the same thing.

"She is really nice," said Ma. "You should meet her. You will like . . . Her mother says she is a very good cook. She has also been brought up in a nice, old-fashioned way. No boyfriends, or any of that nonsense. She will not want to go to work . . . and why should she? Certainly, we have enough money to support a hundred wives. She will stay at home, and she will be good company for me."

This was the problem. Ma appeared to be looking for a wife for herself.

"Ma," said Ramu, "if I want a good cook, I will hire one. I don't think I need to *marry* one. And what difference does it make whether she's had boyfriends or not? I want a wife, not a nun."

"Tcha!" Ma dismissed his words. "All those modern girls you like so much will not settle down properly. They will be too busy taking care of themselves to take care of either you or us. And besides, Ramu, when you get married, you must consider our feelings also. After all, we will all be living together, and your wife will spend more time with me than with you."

This was where Ramu begged to differ, but had still not found the courage to do so vocally. He lived with his parents in a large house. When he'd started working, he had moved out of his childhood bedroom and into a corner suite, with a separate entrance to come and go as he pleased, and joining his parents only for meals. It had worked well for several years, minimizing his housekeeping and maximizing his freedom, but now he suddenly felt as if he were wearing diapers. He wanted to move out, but knew that to raise the topic with his parents was to immediately invoke the reproachful deities of Family Shame and Abandonment. If he moved out after he got married, at least they could direct all their ire and blame on his (as yet unknown) wife.

It was a comforting thought.

His appetite for the vadas faded away. He glanced at his watch. He was supposed to meet some friends at the club later in the evening; perhaps he had time for a quick swim before that.

It was then that she brought up Ashwini.

Ma, of course, didn't refer to her by name, but by antecedents.

"Of course, if you really want modern, there is, as I said, that Desai girl. North-Indian, of course, but vegetarian. Parents are very good people, but the girl, I feel, is too modern."

Ramu heard her out in some confusion. When she'd first mentioned Ashwini's name a week ago, he had dismissed it out of hand. Surely there were better options to be had? But now, he wondered, perhaps there weren't. Maybe those other options would never be better than Wealthy Butt-face and the Virgin Cook.

"She has studied well. She has a good job. She probably does not know how to cook," Ma said, "so she will suit you nicely. Too

modern!" Ma said: "Her mother tells me this girl—this, uh, Ashwini—does not even know that we have spoken about her. She
will get angry, her mother says. What nonsense! But still . . . they
are a good family, so she will adjust. . . . A good family, good
background, and educated, also. There is a cousin," Ma said,
"with a PhD."

"Wow," Ramu said, knowing that he had taken a wrong step.

He made his way thoughtfully to the club swimming pool. It was
his daily habit: to swim thirty placid laps, and he did this
throughout the year, shivering his way through icy winter waters, or ploughing through the hordes of summer children
squealing in the shallows. It was now October, the monsoon
rains had been and gone, and temperatures were rising once
again, for a last late burst of warmth before winter.

As usual for this time of the year, the pool was empty of all
but the group of four elderly men who never seemed to leave.
He paused by the side of the pool, watching them swim. In his
mind, he referred to them as the Buffaloes; they were swaddled
in the fat of a lifetime and wrapped in discolored skin and liked
to immerse themselves in the shallows. They cast vague smiles
in Ramu's direction. On land, the Buffaloes stood transformed
into his parents' so-respectable friends. But in the water they
were part of some strange amphibious species, and Ramu eyed
them dubiously before diving in.

The clear waters of the pool couldn't wash the truth away.
The fact had to be faced: his mother was unleashed and gaining
momentum. In his worst nightmares, of being swept away in a

torrential downpour of maternal enthusiasm, Ramu clung feverishly to his lifeline—he had final veto. He had Final Veto. He had-
Final Veto.

He pulled himself out of the water and headed back to the men's
changing room. His gaze wandered automatically over the long
hair and tight jeans of the young woman standing to one side.
She appeared to be waiting for someone; from the tetchy restlessness of her manner, Ramu guessed it was probably her son.

She couldn't enter, naturally, since the men's changing room
at the club was inviolate; an ode, like Michelangelo's David, to
pristine male nudity, and she seemed to resent her exclusion.
Ramu had heard her speak: he knew her voice to be husky and
melodious, as attractive as the rest of her, but now it changed,
rising quickly up the scale and increasing in volume until she
sounded shrill and irritable.

"Hurry up," she called. "Do you think I have time to waste?
Jaldi! Jaldi!"

He could tell when she became aware of his presence: her
body tensed, and she favored him with a small, tight-lipped smile;
a grudging acknowledgment of distant acquaintance. Ramu nodded back as he walked past, refusing to point out that while the
acquaintance might be grudging, at least on her part—it was far
from distant. He had dated this woman, many years ago. This
was, of course, before she had married—and definitely before her
husband had started working in the same office as Ramu.

Now, the implacable gods of social propriety forced her into a
convenient amnesia, and Ramu humored her, all the while wondering what his colleague would say if Ramu interrupted one of

their business discussions with the information that his wife had once spent an entire evening with Ramu's hand between her thighs.

Nothing more, alas, but those were the days when Ramu and his male friends had been happy with whatever they could get. That was when dates had consisted of the best cheap dinner that one could afford, followed by driving one's car (borrowed for the occasion from some tolerant uncle) furiously to dark corners of the city for dessert: a half hour spent in industriously attempting to explore the Inner Woman. Any inner woman.

That was, in short, when they were twenty, and achieving consensual sex with skittish young women whose knees were pressed tightly together by the weight of Indian morality was a triumph in itself. It had been enough to say:

I've been and gone and done it.

To say: I found a hole and dived right in.

To say: I fucked her. And to dream enviously of their western counterparts; men who, being blessed with women of Easy Virtue, reportedly did their fucking much younger. Eighteen. Sixteen. Fourteen. Twelve. In some countries, the rumor said, they were *born* copulating.

After twenty-five, things changed. The women relaxed, were easier, and suddenly who you slept with became more important than what you did. Quality, dear boy, quality over quantity.

But it was only now, at thirty, that the true Call of the Patriarchy began to make itself felt: the urge to father, to provide, to pay bills for More Than One. Ramu never discussed this with his bachelor friends, for to do so would be to acknowledge the strange conundrum they faced.

For a decade, it seemed, they had been festooned with

women, all sorts, from the cute, the silly, the please-domesticate-mes, to the independent, the fiery, the I'll-sleep-with-but-won't-love-yous, and further beyond, to the Plainly Bizarre. And they had frolicked and gamboled with happy abandon, and no aware-ness of the fate that quietly awaited them: the moment notions of "settling down," marriage, became reality—they found them-selves, absurdly, stuck for choice. All those women, those sillys, those feistys, those Saturday-night-mainstays, had simply van-ished. All of them. Together. Birdlike, in a great migratory move-ment (to somewhere else), these chicks had flown. They had married, dispersed, dehydrated.

The club lawn was festive, with little tables covered in red-and-yellow-checked cloths that fluttered in the evening breeze. Ramu's friends were seated at one of the tables, drinking beer.

"You're late, fucker," said Swamy, "as the man said to his mother-in-law. Have a beer."

"Where's KK?" Ramu asked. "He isn't ditching us, is he?"

"He'll get here eventually," Murthy said. "He must be with that new girlfriend of his."

"Enthu bastard," Swamy said. "He should just bring her here to meet us. Instead of making us wait while he drops her home, and dries her tears, and kisses her good-bye."

Ramu had known these men almost his whole life; they had grown up together, and now he felt a sudden wave of affection towards them. There was Swamy, whose mercurial brilliance Ramu had secretly admired long before the media had made it fashionable to do so. And Murthy, calm, quiet, and who, Ramu occasionally believed, harbored the same well-concealed feelings of hero-worship towards *him*. And the absent KK, of course, always ready with a laugh and a helping hand. Between them, they had achieved a cordial comfort that to some extent, Ramu realized, he would like to replicate in his ideal marriage.

Murthy stared at Ramu's wet hair. "You swam? How come? I thought you usually swim in the mornings."

For a brief, tempting instant Ramu debated the wisdom of sharing his marital plans with his friends—of speaking breezily on the trials of enlisting his mother as a Connubial Pimp intent on trading his economics for the unlimited use of a vagina, a womb, and a free lifetime supply of conversation at cross-purposes—but something held him back. Better perhaps to wait until all the details were in place: the who, the when, the where.

Luckily, their attention was immediately diverted.

"There he is. . . . You know, KK, you're crazy. It's never going to work."

"What?" KK: big, genial, sweating mildly in the late evening sun, chuckling imperviously at Swamy.

"You're wasting your time dating that kid. Cradle-snatching *behenchuth*. She can't be a day older than, what, twenty-two? . . . Beer? Or something else?"

But Ramu could vaguely recognize KK's action for what it was: a fallback position. When you have failed with your generation, you wait for the next one to ripen. Ramu had seen KK's new girlfriend, and she was lovely. If KK dumped her, as he usually did, and he wasn't a married man by then, Ramu wouldn't mind dating her himself—if it weren't for that golden, unarticulated rule: a woman once involved with any of them remained off-limits to his friends.

This kept life simple.

KK refused to respond to Swamy's needling. He just grinned and contented himself with taking a big gulp of beer. Through the desultory conversation that followed, Ramu studied KK's unusual reticence, and was struck by a sudden realization.

KK, perennial dater of women, was serious about this girl.

Serious enough to propose? And be accepted?

And Ramu was enthralled by a startling vision of the future: he and his friends, gentlemen used to wrapping themselves around the nearest beer and saying it with burps—doing so with an assortment of wives about them. A Mrs. KK, a Mrs. Ramu, a Mrs. Murthy, and, god forbid, a Mrs. Swamy.

Mrs. Ramu.

Ramu's mind worried ceaselessly at the elusive cipher those words conjured up, like a dog with a difficult-to-grasp bone. It seemed to him unfair that there should be such a gap between decision and execution—after having resisted matrimony for a decade, surely his very eagerness should now suffice to guarantee an array of suitable women for his selection?

Mrs. Ramu.

Who was going to fill that lacuna in his life?

"There's Ashwini," said Murthy, as though reading his thoughts.

Indeed, there she was. Walking over the lawns towards them.

Ramu felt himself retreating into a watchful, speculative quiet. He focused his attention on Ashwini, observing her manner as she interacted with his friends: a pert reply to Swamy, a wink for KK, her smiling conversation with Murthy. She refused a beer but lit a cigarette, after first checking carefully to see if any of her parents' friends might be about.

She listened with amused delight to the story of KK's nick-name: his real name was Prasad Rao, a name rejected by his friends early in his career in favor of something more colorful. They had finally (over his protests) settled unceremoniously on "Karadi Kundi." Bear-Bottom. Because, said Swamy, his arse, like the rest of him, was big, black, and hairy. Karadi Kundi, KK for short.

Ashwini laughed in all the right places.

She *was* vivacious, attractive, really. Ramu did a quick inventory: she was dressed in a smart jacket and pant ensemble, with—surprise, surprise—thin wire-rimmed glasses on her nose. They gave her an unexpected, agreeably intellectual air. That was good, adding a sobriety to her image that Ramu found pleasing. Her manner with him was easy—he guessed that she still hadn't been told about the discussions between their mothers. She smiled in his direction—and for the first time Ramu wondered: was she attracted to him?

Ramu toyed with that notion for a little while, and found himself disturbingly pleased with it.

Later that night, the delicious prospect of bedding Ashwini was slowly superseded by other considerations.

Of all the women he was considering for a life together, she was undoubtedly the best choice. And yet, and yet, so dreadfully inadequate an option. Ramu knew himself to be well read, deliberate, with, he assured himself, a certain Depth of Purpose that extended beyond foolish, frivolous conversation and endless social preoccupations. Shouldn't there be some compatibility of natures for this sort of thing to work?

Ramu mentally revisited their encounter at the club and

anxiously listed to himself the possible signs of Ashwini's superficiality.

The manner, for instance, in which she coyly insisted on questioning Swamy about his work. Swamy hated small talk about the software company he had founded. It was his baby, not to be trifled with. This was a message that Ashwini, in her social delight, seemed oblivious to.

Her insistence on dropping names, especially names she'd left behind in Bombay.

Her habit of referring to a fat-pocketed bore, whom Ramu despised, as a "dear friend"—instead of, correctly, as a pompous turd accompanied (as such turds often are) by a lot of verbal flatulence.

The unwarranted number of expensive brand labels on her clothes, a type of wanton advertising that Ramu could not condone.

Worst, her anglicized nickname: her close friends, it seemed, called her "Ash," and she encouraged them to do so. Ramu abhorred that: converting a thing of beauty into a thing for western convenience.

Perhaps her nickname provided an apt metaphor for her progress through his mind: Ashwini, the star-like, consort of the sun, rapidly reduced to a lump of dusty carbon residue.

It was his mother, naturally, who first noticed the difference.

A lifetime of training had rendered her excellent at reading Ramu's moods, though somewhat indifferent at interpreting the causes. She gazed at him uneasily at mealtimes and redoubled her energies towards finding him a wife. Ramu sidestepped her efforts and kept his thoughts to himself, as though that might in some way contain them, reduce them, send them packing.

But the depression that had set in kept growing, his desires trapped between his unenthusiastic appraisal of Ashwini (and the even less appealing choices conjured up by his mother) on the one side, and the loneliness that was beginning to whisper through his life on the other. Ramu had long conversations with himself about frying pans and fires, and in the endless watches of the night, knew not which he preferred.

Increasingly, he found himself staying away from dinners at the houses of his married friends. Changing the subject in the face of KK's obvious happiness. Changing television channels in irritation, switching from the mating habits of birds to the hero who found comfort in the arms of a deep-bosomed lovely to, finally, the news, which offered no romance whatsoever.

Occasionally, the scorn he poured on Ashwini's head missed its target and fell, splashing, towards him instead, covering him with self-doubt. Perhaps he was intrinsically unsuited to the quotidian pleasures of marriage?

Inadequate in some way?

The thought wrapped itself depressingly around him until, one day, he decided: it was no use; it was time to call a halt to this whole foolishness.

Time to tell his mother to stop looking.

He never got the chance.

His mother came to the dinner table one evening with the irritated expression of a woman who's been had.

"You are not going to believe this," she said. "I mean, how

could she not tell me? Does this not affect us? Will we not have an interest if you marry that girl? Is it not important?"

Ramu waited patiently for his mother to come to the point.

"You can't marry Ashwini," Ma said, slapping a hot roti down on his father's plate. "Out of the question."

Uh-oh, thought Ramu. She's heard about the dope.

No.

"I mean, I realize she has one left. I am not a fool. But what if that fails? It has been known to happen. Then you will be left a widower, and my grandchildren will be motherless." She answered the question in Ramu's eyes. "It happened two years ago. Ashwini gave away one of her kidneys to a cousin. For a transplant."

Ramu stopped eating.

"I'm not saying that it is not a nice thing to do. But still," Ma said, "of course, we cannot consider her now. Her mother should have told me earlier."

She surfaced once from the ensuing discussion with his father to say consolingly: "Never mind. There are other girls. If you want modern, I will find. I will find lots of modern girls. Don't worry."

KK's engagement party was the usual extravaganza, a mini–wedding reception, with three generations of people stuffing themselves at KK's parents' expense. Chi. Bear-Butt and Sow. *Baby-girl to wed and become Mr. and Mrs. Karadi Kundi.*

Ramu stared at the crowd feeling oddly light-headed. He traced the outlines of his goatee with his thumb and forefinger, sensitive to the transition between smooth, carefully shaved skin and the trimmed outgrowth of hair. He had chosen his clothes with care. He felt the urge in him to make a good impression and he'd catered to it, doing so with a slight, self-aware smile.

He looked for Ashwini. She had to be here. Even if it was just for a short visit, one stop on a series of Saturday-night parties. He had come early, knowing that this was the type of function she would finish first, on her way to something more hip, less sober.

It was three days since he'd decided that she was the woman he wanted to marry. He'd slept on the decision, thought about it while swimming, in the shower, and at work. His reasoning was as clear as could be: what kind of person gives up their kidney to someone else?

Someone with courage.

Someone with conviction.

Someone with principles.

In short, someone with a Depth of Purpose.

Ashwini was a heroine.

This was something he could respect in his wife-to-be, and that others would respect also. The gift of her kidney gave her a depth, and by reflection, him a depth as well.

He'd fought an urge to telephone her—that would not be the right approach. He somehow felt that this first conversation should happen in a milieu they were both used to. A party. This party. They could take it from there. Go somewhere private, if need be.

The fact was, Ramu was not terribly clear on how to proceed. He'd discussed the options with himself. A: He could leave it to the mothers, a choice he'd already dismissed. Far better to circumvent their mothers, talk to Ashwini directly, and then bring the news to his parents as a fait accompli. That would be amusing. B: He could court her as he might any other woman, see where it developed, propose (ring in hand, on his knee) as the grand finale to several months of dating—and suffer, meanwhile, the uncertainty of future rejection. C: He could strike a path somewhere between the first two options: tell her that the mothers were talking—that he himself preferred to deal with such things directly—yes, he was interested—and what did she think?

He tried to untangle himself from one of his father's acquaintances, a gentleman who by day haunted the club swimming pool in the guise of a Buffalo, and who now held tightly on to his arm and repeated with gentle insistence: "*Hanh beta*, so why you don't drop by?"

Ramu stared blindly at the three strands of graying hair combed unconvincingly across the bare stretch of pate. He'd been kidnapped by geriatric perseverance while Ashwini hovered tantalizingly out of sight.

"You come next week. My granddaughter is visiting. From London. You come."

"I will," said Ramu. He wrenched his arm away, helping himself to a kebab from a passing tray.

His companion watched him eat, and then asked querulously, "How it is, this one? Good-uh?"

"Very good," Ramu nodded politely, waiting desperately for the old gentleman to get absorbed in the kebabs, before diving suddenly into the crowd.

* * *

He waved and smiled to passing friends, shaking his head when they waved him over. He felt free, elated, as if a great pressure had lifted. Perhaps they could go for a holiday somewhere before the wedding, he and Ashwini—if the parents didn't prove too great a social barrier to such a plan. Ramu already knew where they were going to live—in that new apartment building in the center of town with the marble floors and the terrace garden.

There they would throw parties where Ashwini will have done Everything. Not just the curtains, or the soufflé. Everything. And Ramu would pour the drinks and look urbane.

A vague anxiety tugged at his brain.

Supposing she said no?

Was it, in fact, better to just trust to the mothers; repose faith in the Great Indian Marriage Machinery?

He tried to convince himself: surely there was more than just his mother to his awareness of himself as being terribly eligible? Yet, he could not deny that he found comfort in the realization that Ashwini, surely, would not have put him (or anyone else) through the same analysis to which he had subjected her.

He couldn't spot her. The crowds were huge. He made his way over to where Swamy was standing by the bar. Ramu forced himself to act casual, hiding his impatience, hugging his secret decision to himself.

"This place," said Swamy, polishing his glasses morosely, "is a fucking zoo. Why that bastard has to go get engaged in this city, I don't know."

"Because he lives here?" suggested Ramu.

"*Chuth.*" Swamy was at his most dogmatic. "What I say is, we go over, kick KK's arse, say hello to his parents, and then fuck off—go to my house, play some music, have a few drinks, relax. Maybe order in some kebab rolls."

He started to move away, oblivious to Ramu's reluctance.

"Where's Murthy," Ramu said idly, trying to delay him.

Swamy began to laugh. "He's driving this chick around."

"What?"

"Driving this chick around, trying to get laid. Denies it, of course. But took her shopping this morning; I rest my case."

"Really." Ramu listened to Swamy with half an ear and scanned the crowds eagerly. Where was she? "Fuck. He must be desperate."

Swamy shrugged, as if to say they had all done such foolish things, and turned away. Ramu said something to him, not moving from the bar, tugging Swamy back like a weak but persistent sea current.

"What?" Swamy turned around.

"Who is she?"

"Who?"

"Murthy's new girlfriend."

"Uh . . . what's her name. That cute chick . . ." Swamy frowned, on the verge, Ramu recognized, of suggesting that for god's sake wasn't this all best discussed over a quiet beer, and could they please get the fuck out of this silk-infested social pigsty? But instead, Swamy abandoned the effort of mentally conjuring up Murthy's love interest with evident relief. "Oh, there they are."

Ramu had stopped listening to him entirely, his attention captured by the woman walking towards him.

Oh there she was.

With a proprietary thrill, Ramu realized that she looked lovely, elegant. It was almost as if she were, like him, dressing especially well this evening. He tried to remain calm, regulating his breath as he might while swimming. Perhaps that was why it took him a few moments to recognize what he was seeing: Ashwini, as women will on such occasions, was wearing a silk saree shot through with gold over a lamé blouse, accessorized with diamond jewelry, an italian handbag, french perfume—and Murthy.

Her voice, when he heard it, was pitched higher than usual. "Hey! Hi, guys!"

Ramu felt a great silence wash through him.

He dared not look at her directly. Murthy, he noticed, was wearing the surprised look of a man who was doubting his own good luck.

Out of the corner of his eye, Ramu saw Ashwini lean across to air-kiss a startled Swamy on both cheeks. She turned to him, doubtless to offer him the same treatment, and from somewhere deep inside him, Ramu found his voice: Swamy and I were just on our way out, he said, stepping away. We'll see you guys later. Coming, Swamy?

As he walked away, a slight smile forced upon his face, he could hear Ashwini say, "You know, this is quite a small affair, really. Engagement parties in Bombay are twice this size."

CLOSED
CURTAINS

Mr. D'Costa lived with his wife in a cul-de-sac off Ulsoor Road, in a pastel pink house that was square and squat and small, with a sloping cement roof and no garden space to speak of. It was identical to the houses that flanked it on either side, except that the others were pastel blue, pastel yellow, and pastel green. They were designed as affordable middle-class housing at a time when Bangalore was small, and everybody lived in houses, and apartments were some sort of unseen exotic Bombay invention. Even today, they spoke of identical resident lifestyles: with windows meshed, barred, and tightly shuttered; with pastel walls scarred and fissured by monsoon rain; the smell of steamed rice idlis and spicy sambar that floated in the air in the mornings; the potted hibiscus plants on the narrow cement footpaths that ran between house and compound wall, interspersed with dusty jasmine and bougainvillea creepers that hugged and further blinded the lower-floor windows in overgrown disarray. The driveways held

Bajaj scooters, and sometimes, perhaps a very old, rarely used Fiat car that had been carefully husbanded over the decades.

There had been more of these houses at one time, lining the lane right up to where it met Ulsoor Road. Thirty-five years ago the area had been considered respectable but certainly not up-market; a good place to bring up a young family. Now, of all the old neighbors, only a few remained: apart from the D'Costas, there were the Ambekars; the Nizamuddins; Mrs. Reddy, relict of the late Wing Cdr. (Ret.) Reddy; the Kuriens next door; and three doors down, the Gnanakan family, where the money that Mrs. Gnanakan painstakingly earned through arranging flowers at minimum expense in her "Daisy" florist shop, her husband discreetly drank away.

The rest of the neighborhood had been swallowed up by the pressures of a growing city. Escalating land prices had nudged the little lane into prime real estate. People had sold their homes and moved further away, leaving behind the detritus: those who didn't have the energy or desire to realize the sudden astonishing worth of their properties and readjust their lives to localities far from the center of town. Grand new bungalows came up on the ruins of the old, inhabited by people who air-dashed to delhi-london-tokyo so often, they had no time for friendly neighbor-hood pursuits. Witness the Lakshminarayanans and the Jaffers, who, between them, had bought and converted five of the old houses into two palaces that now guarded the mouth of the little lane in stately fashion. Mr. D'Costa wouldn't dream of dropping in on them for a chat and a cup of tea, as he might with Mrs. Ambekar or anyone else of the old brigade. They probably wouldn't even know who he was, so he left well alone, stealing occasional glimpses of their lives by peeping into their gardens as he walked to the Ulsoor Market, and chatting with their servants as they scurried to and from work or came to buy fresh bread from the Good Fellows Bakery man.

Since his retirement ten years earlier, Mr. D'Costa liked to regard himself as a Neighborhood Elder. It gave him a sense of purpose, and rendered meaningful his habit of standing at an upstairs window and conducting a detailed survey of his neighbors in a still, intense manner, born of lingering time and low energy.

He would follow this up by popping out of his house to hold discourse several times a day. He timed his trips to the vegetable market to coincide with the hapless Mrs. Gnanakan's morning walk, gleaning plump morsels of pumpkin and information about her husband's drinking habit with equal efficiency. His scooter would get its daily wipe just when the Good Fellows Bakery man trundled down the lane on his bicycle, balancing the big metal bin full of bread, currant buns, shortbread biscuits, and mutton puffs behind him. As the neighborhood ammas and ayahs, the madams and maids, collected around, Mr. D'Costa abandoned his scooter to gather news and confirm his sightings of the morning.

"Your husband not well, Mrs. Ambekar? Didn't go to office this morning . . ." That's right, Mr. D'Costa, he has a cold.

"*Yenu*, Muniamma, *amma nimage* salary *eevage kodalilava?*" No, sir, she hasn't paid me my salary yet. Late as usual, and how do I settle my children's school fees?

More important, he dispensed information on what everyone else was doing, and with whom, discussing neighborhood matters with a weighty sense of deliberation that always impressed his listeners. Personal questions addressed to him, though, were always answered with a brisk, uninformative, "Fine! Very fine!" Everyone knew that Mrs. D'Costa lived a subterranean life deep in the recesses of their bungalow; she rarely surfaced for any kind of social dialogue. It was even rumored that she had succumbed to some terrible forgetful dementia; if that was true, Mr. D'Costa never confirmed it.

Of all the changes that had taken place in the neighborhood, the block of flats opposite his house proved the most interesting. It was a large, three-story building painted a gleaming white, surrounded by green lawns and colorful cultivated flower borders— the product of a real-estate developer's zeal and the purchased remains of three square bungalows. The inhabitants were not inaccessibly wealthy, yet they were fascinatingly different from anything Mr. D'Costa knew. He'd read about them in *India Today* magazine. Something about the new young professionals and their cosmopolitan lifestyle.

"Puppies," he explained to an astonished Mrs. Reddy. Or guppies. He couldn't remember which. From his research, he knew that the apartment building contained two people in the software industry, a tax consultant, an oncologist at the glamorous, recently built Modi Hospital on Airport Road, a German engineer, a Lipton's man, and in the ground-floor flat directly opposite, an investment banker married to an advertising professional.

It was the last couple who succeeded in fully capturing Mr. D'Costa's migratory interest. The banker, Aman Kapur, and his copywriting wife, Rohini.

He'd noticed them the day they'd moved in: young, very

young, as he had once been, but utterly different in their ways. They were as Indian as he was, but they had about them the strangeness of an inexplicable foreign movie. It wasn't just the matching clothes: both husband and wife were clad in shorts and T-shirts, which looked nice on him, but skimpy on her. It wasn't the quality of the richly upholstered furniture that was being carried in piece by expensive piece. It wasn't the large shiny car painted black, with jazz music blaring through the open doors. It wasn't the way they laughed together, or even the appallingly casual manner in which they held hands on a public road, without once being aware of the impropriety of it all.

Mr. D'Costa was instantly enthralled. After years of even-handed interest around the neighborhood, he found his attention increasingly tugged across the street, right into the Kapur apartment. His favorite perch at the upstairs window gave him a delightful bird's-eye view straight through their French windows, directly into their sitting room, and, if he squinted hard, to the conjoined dining room beyond. He quickly learned the rhythm and flow of the household opposite, the arrivals, the departures, when they rose and when they slept.

For a long time, they kept to themselves, as did the other people in that apartment building. They didn't have a housewarming party for the neighbors, or bring trays of sweets around the lane to introduce themselves. They just moved in and started their life, which, in the beginning, didn't seem to center around their flat at all. They were rarely at home; both of them worked all day, and then frequently went out again in the evening.

When they did stay home, that was the signal for Mr. D'Costa to settle by his window seat, watching. At mealtimes, he studied the distant dishes on their dining table, wondering what food they contained. The same Goan meen curry and vegetables that he ate, or something impossibly foreign and romantic? He wondered what it was they discussed when they sat around with their jean-clad friends in the drawing room, or in the sunken garden, drinks in hand and listening to the harsh, too-loud music that seemed to have neither melody nor delicate rhythm and whose volume was finally tempered several months later by the baby's arrival. Fragments of conversation wafting across the road revealed unabashed Americanisms in what had previously been unquestioned English territory: "That's great!" instead of "Lovely!"; "Cool!" and "Awesome!" for "Good show!" Nice guys had replaced good chaps.

And through it all, the hand-holdings and the hugs and the kissing hello and kissing good-bye, in full view of the neighbors, who, it was increasingly apparent, didn't really exist or matter to this couple.

It was a fascination that did not wane.

Late in her pregnancy, to Mr. D'Costa's delight, Rohini Kapur gave up her job and made her first appearance as a neighborhood memsahib. She liked to stroll heavy-footed down the little lane in her new avatar, taking in the slumberous leafy world she lived in, smiling politely at all the neighbors who, for months now, she had seen only as blurs through her car window. It took Mr. D'Costa two days to introduce himself, and one more week to gently entice her into his information net.

"Ah, Mrs. Kapur," he would say. "Not buying bread today?"

Not today, Mr. D'Costa.

"Your husband is not eating bread-toast for breakfast?"

Yes, yes, he does. Toast and coffee.

"I see. I see. . . . Where he is working? Bank, no? . . . Good job, uh?"

Quite good, Mr. D'Costa. He likes it, anyway.

"And your good health? You are . . . keeping well?"

Very well, thank you.

"Very good. Very good. Right-o, then."

Try as he might, Mr. D'Costa could feel no chord of similarity between the life the Kapurs led and his own long-ago, mustily re-membered youth. It went beyond mere cultural differences; of times then and times now.

Mr. D'Costa remembered: the treats of his boyhood were to munch on Huntley Palmer biscuits and to visit the cinema; the goals of early manhood never transcended a burning desire to dress and act like an English gentleman. To have the grand good fortune to study in England, and perhaps the ultimate blessing of being able to make a home there, or perhaps in Australia or even America. They had tried so hard and so faithfully to cross all those impossible cultural bridges—shyly, self-consciously feeling out the way; diffident of their Indian habits, of their accents, of the way their wives spoke English.

It had been a time, he remembered, when the prized jobs were still in the plantation companies, run by British bosses who retained their power and their membership to whites-only clubs, unswayed, even after Independence. When it had still helped to have a name like Peter D'Costa, and not, like his colleague, Na-gendra Pani, whose moniker their English superiors had brutally shortened to Nag. And made jokes about it, too.

Now what was he to make of these youngsters across the road, who acted with all the assurance of a people who have forsaken those jewel-bright foreign jobs that feverishly glisten and beckon from across the oceans, siren whispers that taunt you in your dreams; forsaken those jobs to return to their country with an ease and an air that indicates that this is perhaps not a very big thing to do at all. My goodness, Mr. D'Costa. My word.

Vaguely he had known, through reading the papers and the magazines, that things had changed in this country. But this, opposite, was proof.

Every now and then he shared the information he gleaned with the other older neighbors, but in a most casual way, never revealing the depths of his interest in the Kapurs, or the duration he spent gazing into their living room from his hidden niche by the window. To ward off further inquiry into his methods, he sometimes said that the Kapurs lived a life that was utterly familiar to him.

"Like my son," he said, to Mrs. Nizamuddin. "In Australia."

"Like my daughter," she said, quick as a flash. "In London." But there Mr. D'Costa had his doubts. Mrs. Nizamuddin's daughter was married to a young man whom Mrs. Nizamuddin carefully referred to as a chef, which sounded to Mr. D'Costa's ears like *chess* pronounced through a toothless mouth, *che-ff,* but which he knew to mean nothing more than a cook. And what kind of a profession was that? Mr. D'Costa's son, he never failed to remind her, was an MBA.

"And like my daughter too," said Mr. Kurien irrelevantly. His daughter lived up the road and held no mysteries for Mr. D'Costa. She had chosen to disregard her parents' views and marry an inappropriate young man in a headstrong, falling-in-love way, a proceeding that, as Mr. D'Costa said, was always filled with foolishness.

He wanted to discuss this changing-times business with his wife. Once, she would have been interested in such topics, her alert mind composing some acerbic comment on the absurdity of youngsters the world over that would make him laugh and give him comfort. But her declining brain rarely took an interest in anything these days; conversation between them had slowed and finally trickled to a stop. They had turned away from each other, his eyes actively roaming over his neighborhood and the retired world he knew, hers increasingly fixated by the television set and the Cartoon Network. The bright colors and simple plots kept her riveted. Unlike other channels, it didn't seem to matter that her mind wandered, and her eyes weakened. She was also getting increasingly deaf, and Mr. D'Costa was chased all over his house by extra-loud shrieks and thuds of animal mayhem, by music that jumped and giggled with crazy glee.

He attended to the household matters: did the shopping, went to the bank to deposit their dividends and pension payments, supervised the plumbers and electricians who routinely battled to preserve the increasingly decrepit house, and paid Sakamma the ayah, who for ten years had cleaned and cooked and stolen what she could. Now and then he'd look in on his wife, but she barely noticed, her eyes on the screen, her face bizarrely painted in the yellows and blues thrown by the TV into the darkened room, her lower jaw moving rhythmically over a toothless mouth whose dentures reposed unused in a muddy glass of water by her bed.

The doctor said that he should expect such decline to continue. As yet, no cure was available. As time went on, the doctor said, she would recognize less and less of her life. Mr. D'Costa did not reply that the gradual erasure of his wife had rendered his own life unrecognizable as well.

Through the years, they had roused themselves, the D'Costas, to read and discuss the letters dutifully mailed to them once a month by their son, with whom they had been blessed late in life and after two years of saying Hail Marys three times a day and sometimes in their sleep. Now Mr. D'Costa read the letters to himself, sharing the news with the pastel walls of his house. He too was an investment banker, their son, just like Aman Kapur, but settled with a foreign wife and two children whom they had never seen in Australia. There was no question, financially speaking, of Mr. D'Costa paying for a ticket to Australia, and no question, it appeared, of their son bringing his family to visit them. Mr. D'Costa tried not to be hurt. No doubt his son would come when he could. After all, didn't he sometimes send money along with the letter, his son? A sizable amount, perhaps as much as twenty Australian dollars, which Mr. D'Costa would convert at the bank and happily add the four hundred or so rupees to his account.

There was a deep kernel of truth in what he'd told the neighbors. In his heart of hearts he felt sure that the life his son led in Australia couldn't be all that different from what he saw across the road. His son and his son's wife, Elizabeth, both working; his grandchildren being looked after by god-knows-whom. When she was not working, his son wrote, Elizabeth cooked dinners and played golf and tennis at the club. All of which was apparently why she was always too busy, too tired, to write or send them pictures of their grandchildren.

But that was the life his son preferred. And Mr. D'Costa consoled himself that times had changed, even though that fact seemed to have escaped Mrs. Amberkar's son, a chartered accountant who dutifully lived with his parents, and whose wife was expecting their second grandchild, as Mrs. Ambekar reminded everyone with distressing frequency. It was with no small sense of irritation that Mr. D'Costa found himself frequently plunged into daydreams where his own son did the same, and he could take his grandchildren with him to the Ulsoor vegetable market.

Mr. D'Costa found himself staring across the road, with worry etched upon his face. He was not alone. A group of neighbors stood with him, and seemed to share his concern.

"Why don't you go across and inquire, Mr. D'Costa?"

"Yes, yes, something is definitely wrong, Mr. D'Costa. That nice young girl. Good mother. Such a sweet baby she has. As pretty as my own granddaughter."

"Where is the husband? I did not see him. Traveling, is it?"

Mr. D'Costa paid the Good Fellows Bakery man and wondered what to do. He stared across the street for possibly the tenth time, eyeing Rohini Kapur's curtained windows with some concern. They were usually thrown open at first light, to let in the fresh sweet early morning air. The uncharacteristic closed curtains this morning weren't the only signs of something wrong. The lights had been on late in the Kapur house last night. Not a party or anything. Just these two women talking and talking by the open balcony doors. Rohini and her friend, that rather alarming Miss Tara Srinivasan, who dashed about carelessly dressed with her long hair flashing, uncombed, in the wind. Nothing to put his finger on really—women, he knew, had this remarkable ability to talk their whole lives through—nothing to engender this vague feeling of unease—except that the first bottle of wine had given way to a second, and then he had seen her cry. Rohini, weeping a deep sorrow into the lap of her friend.

Mr. D'Costa concluded that it was probably some matter of husband and wife. Certainly, those hugs and kisses, so improperly given at meetings and good-byes, had fallen away many months ago. But that too was natural after the birth of a child. The women got testy and tired, and were best left to revive.

Mr. D'Costa had missed his usual nightly treat of watching an old-timer movie after his wife departed for bed, movies that took him back to a time when he had been young enough and fool enough to think that yes, someday, he too would be a Jimmy Stewart, a Cary Grant, a Master of the Universe. Instead he had stayed by the window, shirtless and in a banian vest in the cool evening breeze.

And this morning, closed curtains.

He wondered what to do. Perhaps she was not well; perhaps there was no one to attend to her, since her husband was out of town. The servants, after all, couldn't be counted on in a time of trouble. They always seemed to choose the moments when you needed them most to come and complain about their own miserable lives.

Perhaps he should go across and inquire. After all, hadn't he helped her once before? Hadn't he been there to support her when she was most in need? *A help in need is a help in deed.* And, good woman that she was, she saw to it that he never had cause to regret it, by treating him ever after with a certain special courtesy and respect that came from her eyes and made him feel proud and important and included in her life. It had all happened, he remembered, rather suddenly.

Rohini Kapur had reached the end of her pregnancy. Her baby was due in just three weeks. Her short, sprightly body had grown bulbous and huge, seemingly overwhelmed by the weight it carried. "Kind of like a back-to-front turtle," she would joke, when Mr. D'Costa asked her how she was feeling. Certainly she was unrecognizable as the young woman of compact energy she had once been. She had taken to spending long hours sitting on her balcony in front of the French windows, sipping at fruit juices and reading novels and simply staring at the flowers in the garden, her eyes dulled and restless, captured by the nervous tick that kept a countdown on her ongoing pregnancy.

Mr. D'Costa spied her sitting on her balcony, her head bent over a book, as he left his house to walk the short distance to Ulsoor Market for his daily shopping. Her distant presence triggered a fresh outbreak of the irritation that had plagued him since the previous day. It had been most annoying. He'd watched Rohini busy herself at the dining table with bread, butter, slices of tomato, cucumber, lettuce, and cheese, and he could not resist informing everyone, when they were all gathered around the Good Fellows Bakery man. "Every day she is eating sandwiches for lunch, you know."

"Is that so? Just sandwiches, is it? Nothing hot, is it? Tchi, tchi," said Mrs. Ambekar, for whom lunch had to be hot and homemade, preferably millet bhakdi breads, eaten with hot lentil and legume stews like amti-pitle, vegetables, and a nice pickle, like that spicy gongura that Mrs. Reddy used to make and send over, though not as frequently since her husband died, poor soul. Sandwiches, dry, raw, and inhospitable, were not food enough for one, let alone for two.

But it was Mrs. Gnanakan, who usually agreed with him on all matters, who had said: "No, no, Mr. D'Costa. How can that be? You must be mistaken."

And Mr. D'Costa wanted to say, with an irritation that refused to fade even one day later: Who are you to question me about these people? Do I not know them as if they were my own children? Would not Elizabeth have eaten similar sandwiches while carrying his grandchildren?

It was, oddly enough, that very irritation that almost made him miss the once-in-a-lifetime opportunity. He stepped out of his house with a plastic woven basket on his arm and an old cricket cap on his head, his head so steeped in annoyance that he almost walked twenty yards before he heard the panic-stricken voice, calling from behind him: Mr. D'Costa! He shuddered later to think that, a few yards more, and he would have missed hearing Rohini's voice completely, thereby leaving the final honors to Mr. Kurien or someone else.

Instead, it was he who had the pleasure of announcing to Mr. Kurien across the wall, and subsequently to everyone else as well, that he had actually visited the Kapur home.

That he had helped Rohini out at a very crucial moment, just as a father would.

As a prospective grandfather would.

The facts are thus: with Aman Kapur on a business trip and due back the next day, the cook out shopping, the telephone choosing this moment (of all moments) to cross connect and go on the blink, preventing Rohini from calling anyone else, and the baby rushing down with a hasty disregard for anyone else's timetable, Rohini did the only thing she could. She hailed Mr. D'Costa.

He rushed to her side, his alarm and helplessness dying down before her own.

He couldn't drive her car. The last time he had got behind a steering wheel was twenty years ago, and that had been in an Ambassador car, very different from the fancy new piece that reposed in Rohini's garage in the building basement. So he walked quickly to the main street and flagged down an autorickshaw. They both squeezed into the back, with Mr. D'Costa awkwardly clinging onto the small suitcase that Rohini had providentially packed just the previous day, and bounced off towards the maternity hospital. The auto-driver rose gamely to the occasion and drove even more like a film star than ever, and the auto lurched and bumped its way through every pothole, unwittingly hastening the birth process to an alarming extent. As soon as they arrived, Rohini was surrounded by her doctor and attendant nurses and rushed off to the labor room, and Mr. D'Costa breathed again.

He called her mother, in a two-minute call to Delhi, from the IST/STD telephone booth outside.

He called her friend, Miss Tara, a little nervously, but thankfully got only Tara's mother.

He couldn't call Aman Kapur because Rohini had left the number behind, and he couldn't afford to pay for the call to Singapore anyway.

He then bought a box of *mithai*, sweetmeats steeped in sugar and ghee and celebration, with the last of his vegetable money and waited outside the labor room.

Every now and then, a nurse would step out and tell him that his granddaughter was doing well, and that everything was as it should be.

By six o'clock, the baby was still not born, but the waiting had changed in its very character. Rohini's mother had caught the first plane out of Delhi and was now inside the labor room with her daughter, stepping out only very occasionally with tear-reddened eyes that had cried at her daughter's pain, to say things like "*Arrey baba,* more ice cubes!" Rohini's friend Tara waited silently on a chair, fidgeting and clearly itching to be inside with her friend. Other acquaintances and friends dropped by to check on her progress; they stayed awhile and then left, promising to return as soon as they heard of the baby's delivery. Aman had finally been contacted by Tara, who had spent a full hour inside that ISD/STD booth, and he was arriving into Bangalore in the middle of the night.

Amidst all these people, Mr. D'Costa's presence was indeed redundant. And so he went home, leaving the box of mithai behind.

The first time Mr. D'Costa saw the baby was about a week after the delivery, and shortly after Rohini had returned home from the hospital. He waited until he thought that she and her mother and her baby would be well settled after the shift and then decided to pay a visit.

He dressed carefully, and crossed the road, feeling absurdly nervous. It was the first time that he was paying a social visit to a place of which he felt he knew every sacred detail.

He paused outside the Kapur apartment door and frowned.

He could hear the noise and chatter of many visitors inside. How had he missed their arrival? No doubt because of the time he had spent getting himself ready.

Later, when he dwelt upon his visit, it was with great clarity, a series of scenes from the cinema.

He remembered entering that drawing room—not full of aunts and uncles and people of his generation as he had expected, but instead a whole brood of youngsters, friends of the new parents.

Overload.

Mr. D'Costa remembered his confidence faltering, and then Rohini's blessed face, lighting up and moving towards him in that crowd. He focused in on her. Physically, she was still overblown and bloated, but there was a lightness in her eyes, that earlier, long-forgotten energy gusting out of her in waves.

"Please," she said. "Come. Meet my husband."

And then her handsome husband, that so very smart young man whom he was meeting for the first time, shaking Mr. D'Costa by the hand and looking serious and yet smiling and thanking him for looking after his wife while he was away, and won't he please take a seat and have a drink?

A drink.

Mr. D'Costa hadn't had more than an infrequent glass of beer in a very long time. He was sufficiently relaxed by his warm reception to consider the offer seriously. He could sense the eyes of the other youngsters in the room on him, but when he turned around they were all smiling pleasantly enough; one of them quickly vacated an armchair for him. Perhaps they had all been told the story of his adventure with Rohini.

A drink. Aman was already moving towards the elaborate

bar, and the whisky bottle that lay open on it. It was barely
teatime, but everyone was in a celebratory mood. Mr. D'Costa
caught sight of the label on the bottle and almost gasped. It—lying so casually open, as though it were nothing more than a bottle of water—was one of the most expensive whisky brands in
the world. A rare single malt that, Mr. D'Costa quickly calcu-
lated, would cost around five thousand rupees even if one were
to pick it up in the cheapest duty-free. He had read about it, and
had always thought it the province of men who lived large and
well and had their pictures taken with beautiful women on the
cover of magazines. Five thousand rupees. That was fully as
much as he received from a month's worth of dividends.

He thought: How much money do these youngsters have?

And: Yes, he would most certainly like to have that drink.

He remembered Rohini putting her hand on his arm, and
saying: But first you must come and see the baby.

He nodded dutifully and followed her into the guest bedroom. The baby's cot, she explained, had been moved from their
bedroom upstairs into the room below, where her mother, and
now Rohini, slept. This was to ensure that Aman wasn't dis-
turbed in the night, while she and her mother took turns with
the baby. Mr. D'Costa nodded understandingly. After all, the
man had to go out to work every day, and that was difficult to do
on interrupted sleep.

And where is your dear mother? he asked.

Out shopping for baby clothes, said Rohini. She should be
back soon.

And Mr. D'Costa was angry with himself for not noticing her
departure either. He felt that his visit was most ill-timed. He
couldn't help notice that the volume level in the drawing room

had increased since he left it. There was really no question about it: his presence was a damper on that youthful crowd. They were getting boisterous again, and loud snatches of their conversation came into the guest room where the little bundled baby slept undisturbed. Mr. D'Costa couldn't help listening. It was simply his habit to do so.

He heard a male voice say, somewhat pedantically: ". . . so after much discussion, we concluded that labor pain was like getting kicked in the balls."

"Fuck!" said a second man. "Come on, Farhan. *Nothing* can be that bad!"

"And why not?" said a woman, speaking indignantly. "It probably is a lot worse!"

"It *is* a lot worse" came Farhan's voice, dryly. "By inference, being in labor for a whole day and night, like Rohini, must be like getting kicked in the balls, without a break, *for twenty-four hours straight.*"

There was a visceral sucking-in of breath by all the men present, and Mr. D'Costa too could feel a responsive quiver run through him at the thought. He was appalled and fascinated by the frankness of the conversation (no ladies and gentlemen these, for all that they were apparently well brought up), and forced his attention back to the baby, helpless cause of her mother's carnage.

He made all the appropriate noises while his mind pondered: stay for a drink of a lifetime and impose some more, or leave while they were still pleased to see him?

The decision was taken out of his hands entirely.

He exited the baby's room with Rohini, his mind still undecided between temptation and dignity, when the front door opened and Rohini's mother swept in, followed by the houseboy struggling under an armful of packages.

She nodded amiably to the greetings of her daughter's friends, and then spied Mr. D'Costa. The immediate joy on her face made it clear: if there was one person who believed that, without him, Rohini would have faced the direst of times, this was she.

"Mr. Dacosta! . . . So nice! . . . So kind! . . . I wanted to drop in and thank you personally, but so busy with the newborn baby!"

He was involuntarily swept back into the baby's room to admire again the newborn infant while she pointed out with pride the reproduction of her son-in-law's nose and her daughter's fingers. "Maya," she said. "We are going to call her Maya."

Mr. D'Costa was back in his familiar milieu. There were no mysteries here.

"Come, Mr. Dacosta." She led him back to the drawing room, and asked, "Now please have something . . ."

"I'm just fixing him a drink," Aman put in.

"Ichi! Aman! A drink at four o'clock in the afternoon! Nah, nah. What will Mr. Dacosta think! He is not a drunken one like all you people!" She shook her head affectionately at the chorus of halfhearted denials. "Mr. Dacosta will prefer some hot tea and some nice *garam-garam* snacks."

Temptation was swept away on a tide of goodwill; he saw his drink vanish into someone else's hands and drunk thereafter as though it was the merest home-brew, and Mr. D'Costa found himself meekly agreeing to tea and hot samosas.

He ate three samosas with chutney, which were indeed delicious, and drank two cups of well-sugared tea. Rohini's mother sat by his side, and kept his plate filled, and his mouth engaged in exchanging all manner of information crucial to their understanding of each other. He found himself telling her about his son in Australia, and his long-ago job of forty years with British Tobacco. Just so would he have liked to sit across from Elizabeth's mother, chatting pleasantly about their grandchild and the commingling of their families.

The back of his mind, however, couldn't help questioning, over and over: how much money did these youngsters make?

Surely, surely, it was enough for a plane ticket?

And today, several months later, closed curtains.

"You know them so well," said Mr. Kurien, without intentional malice, "why don't you go and check?"

Mr. D'Costa ignored both Mr. Kurien and his own impulses and waited. But when the curtains remained defiantly closed the following morning as well, he decided to act.

He told himself that he had to go vegetable shopping anyway; it was just a question of stopping en route, a small meaningless diversion, nothing more. He imagined: perhaps Rohini would turn to him, to cry and confide her problems. Perhaps, once again, he was to be her support in distress, what with his son out of town, her parents living in Australia, and all.

As once before, he dressed carefully, shaving and bathing and then drying his hair before combing it through with Brylcreem. He ironed the blue-and-pink checked polyester shirt and light blue poplin pants that constituted one of his best attires. He dressed slowly, then removed the pure leather brown belt from the plastic bag at the back of his cupboard. He looped it around his waist and slipped his feet into black crisscrossed Bata sandals. He was ready.

He looked in on his wife and told her he was heading out to the market. He half hoped that she would comment on his dress, but as usual, she barely paid attention. Her gaze was fixed on the television screen, where a pert-looking cartoon girl dressed in an animal skin stood with arms akimbo. *"But, Fred . . . !"* went the nasal twang. *"Oh, brother!"* His wife smiled in response and raised the volume. Mr. D'Costa closed the door behind him as he left.

It could be nothing. Perhaps Rohini was just sleeping late after a party. Perhaps she had left for a trip while Mr. D'Costa had been away to the market. Perhaps she had changed her housekeeping style. What, after all, were closed curtains? It could be nothing.

He had to ring the bell three times before it was answered. And then, immediately, he knew his impulses had been correct.

The door swung open to reveal a darkened, unkempt house. Rohini looked devastated. In fact, she *was* devastated. Something dreadful had happened in her life, causing her eyes to redden and swell, her skin to blotch, her T-shirt to crumple and stain, and leaving her hair greasy, uncombed, and in tangled disarray.

Mr. D'Costa's mind darted about in horror. What could have caused this? An erring husband? An upset with her mother-in-law? A problem with her baby? His grandchildren? Why had his son's letters made no mention of this?

A thousand questions bubbled up inside him, but they all died before they found speech, quelled by the unexpected, implacable impatience in her eyes. The eyes of his daughter-in-law, repulsing him. He felt himself falter. What did he really know of the alien being who stood before him?

"Mrs. Kapur," Mr. D'Costa finally found refuge in formality. "Please excuse, but. . . . Your house . . . everything, is it okay?"

What happened? Where are your servants? Your baby? *What happened to you?*

The ghost of a smile on Rohini's face was not echoed in her voice, as she answered the questions he could not voice. "The baby is at my mother's house in Delhi, and the servants are on leave."

And your husband?

But there was no further explanation.

It appeared she was waiting for him to leave.

Mr. D'Costa wandered back into the street, tightly clutching his plastic shopping bag. The gleaming white apartment building reared up behind him, and he kept his back to it, resolutely facing the pastel pink house from which he came. His gaze rested on the dark trails that edged the top of the walls. Every monsoon lengthened these trails, the rain dragging the dirt of the roof down with it, in filthy fat tears that coated the house in relentless, ever-narrowing stains until it looked like blackened fungal icing on pink cake. A long time ago, Mr. D'Costa had asked his son for a few extra dollars to repaint the house. If the money arrived soon, perhaps he would paint the house white this time. Or perhaps he wouldn't repaint at all, for, pink or white, the rain would surely strike again and again.

Mr. D'Costa felt a dismay creep through his body, but before he could dwell on it, he sighted a familiar neighborhood figure turning the corner.

"Oh, Mrs. Gnanakan," he called, and walked briskly over to inquire about her husband's state of health.

TWO FOUR
SIX EIGHT

Mary and Mrs. Rafter died within a week of each other. I learned about Mrs. Rafter's demise from the *Old Girls' Newsletter.* "May she rest in pece," it said beneath her photograph, quaintly and hurriedly, or perhaps simply in wry acknowledgment that she would never rest in peace. The blurb went on to mention her forty years of devoted service; the scar tissue resulting thereby still evident, no doubt, in two generations of old school girls.

Mary had no such obituary. The news of her death was brought to us by her daughter, Rosamma, a few days after it happened, along with an unstated hope that her former employers might wish to do something for Mary's family.

"Give this woman something," said my brother Ramu, "and get rid of her."

"Poor thing," said my mother. "She was not so old to die. Not well, is it? You are a naughty sweetie baby."

Rosamma dutifully crooned to the child on my mother's lap. "Baby-amma," she said. "Baby-ammu-kutty. Yes, Ma," she said. "She was very sick. So we took her to the government hospital, they gave some injection, she died, Ma."

"Terrible . . . See, what plump legs she has."

Rosamma plucked at the baby's thigh with her fingers and kissed them. She held her hands out, but I got there before she could take the child from my mother.

Rosamma was the spitting image of Mary. Short, sturdy, as dark as the bark on the shemaram tree, the strength of ten elephants quiescent in her arms.

Rosamma, dressed in a white saree bordered with blue, long dark hair oiled and twisted into a tight bun at the back of her neck, funereal, rice-christianized, radiating competence and the warm smell of sun-baked skin that cannot afford to bathe more than three times a week, squatted at my mother's feet and smiled up at me as I carefully gathered my child into my arms.

I could not bring myself to smile back.

Too much like her mother, Rosamma was.

Mary first came to us when I was three. The previous ayah had been dismissed by my mother in a fit of temper. For four days afterwards, my mother muttered and scolded. "That lying good-for-nothing!" she would say, as she dragged a comb painfully through my hair. "That thieving mongrel, taking advantage of my goodness, just like everybody else. Who else will let her get away with so much, tell me? Hurry up, do you think I have time for nothing else?" And her palm would smack me hard across the arm in her impatience to get me ready. On the fifth day, she relaxed. "Such a problem, finding a good servant," she told my father. "But I think this one will do. She looks clean and polite."

I missed my old ayah and stared resentfully at this replacement, refusing to go to her when she sat on the floor and smiled and tried to tempt me into her arms. I hid behind my mother, and heard her say:

"She doesn't like you. I thought you said you were good with children."

She'll come to me, Ma, Mary said. She'll come.

"We'll see," said my mother. "If she doesn't settle with you quickly, I can't pay you so much."

Mary was engaged at a hundred rupees a month, as much, in those days, as my mother spent on a cotton saree. Far more, as my mother unfailingly pointed out, than she would get any where else. I ended up clasped in her arms before the day was through, sucking on the sweet that had tempted me there, and she stayed with us for years, turning quickly into an extension of my body, her smell as familiar to me as my own.

By the time I was ten, however, I didn't need her for much. I dressed, bathed, and fed myself. She no longer slept on the floor beside my bed at night, wrapped in an old sheet like a soon-to-be-burned corpse. I wouldn't be shushed, I didn't listen when she scolded. Instead, I learnt to scold her back, carelessly, imitating my mother's voice and querulous intonation.

Mary, to me, was nothing. I had other, more important things to think about—like school. That was all I talked about at home, school, chattering to my mother, ignoring everything else. In the afternoons, when my mother rested on her bed under the slow-soughing fan that gently stirred the stewy summer heat, Mary squatted on the floor by her side, massaging her feet. I didn't notice that, every afternoon, Mary's strong dark hands eased the pain out of my mother's ankles and, at the same time, massaged her opinions about me deep into my mother's skin.

It is a shame, she said, that missy does not like the tasty food you are putting on the table. So much effort you put, one bite in this house is worth ten in others, but when you are not at home, missy complains of it to me.

And: It is a shame that missy does not learn your good manners. See how she speaks to the cook. I don't mind, what else do I live for but to serve this family, but the cook is threatening to quit if she shouts at him again.

Lately, I could not even ask Mary to bring me a glass of water without my mother saying: "Go bring it yourself. You have legs. Use your legs as much as you do your mouth."

I would sulk, but briefly, my attention wandering immediately back to the most important place on earth, school, where even parents, when they visited, had to be attentive, mind their manners, and pay attention to what was said.

School was where we went to get a "convent education," which meant, as far as I could tell, learning mathematics, English, geography, history, science, Hindi, a choice of Sanskrit OR French OR Kannada, singing, painting, How to Be English, and How to Be Good. The last two items were not officially on the syllabus, but there was no mistaking their importance. School was founded a hundred years previously, by the English church, for little English girls residing in the army cantonment of Bangalore. The English had left, but their ghosts remained.

Fee-fi-fo-fum
Kiss the arse of the Englishman

It was a curious puzzle, one that I never resolved. Be proud of your country, they said. Democratic. Republic. Independent. And be proud of the English traditions of your school. Remember the greatness of Indians dead, they said: Mahatma Gandhi, Akbar-Ashoka-Chandragupta, and use your fork, not your fingers. No, my girl, *we* don't call it the Sepoy Mutiny; for us, it was the First War of Independence, and if the Queen of England were to see you slouching like that, would she be pleased? Even the slightest infraction of rules meant scoldings, and a loss of house points.

In retrospect I suppose at least some of the trouble could have been avoided if I hadn't been late that particular day. I could have stood in my proper place during chapel services, right between Tara and Freny, and Tara would have handed me the note directly. Instead of which, I remained at the back along with the other latecomers, next to Mrs. Rafter, whose malignant eyes magnified the slightest infraction. Tara's note was passed in my direction through the softly moving hands of several girls, one of whom opened it, read it, and kept it in shocked delight.

To turn it in, the very next day, to the last place on earth that notes passed in chapel should go, directly to Mrs. Rafter.

Of course, being late to school that morning was not my fault. If Mary hadn't spoiled my uniform, I would have been on time. She didn't spoil my uniform by accident, either. The scorch marks left on my shirt by the iron were painstakingly achieved.

The previous evening my mother had returned from the stores and dropped her handbag on her bed before going to the hall to make a telephone call.

I waited patiently for her to slide deep into conversation with her friend. This was usually good for at least twenty minutes. I had plenty of time. I walked softly to the bedroom and slipped inside.

Mary had beaten me to it. There she was, her hand deep inside my mother's purse.

This purse was a magnet for all the dependants in the house. My mother would go shopping, and then carelessly leave it lying around her bedroom while she had a cup of tea out on the verandah, or discussed menus with the cook. She never remembered to check the contents or to keep it locked.

The servants presumably used that money to feed their children. My brother and I used it for play. Once a week, my mother pressed a ten-paisa coin into my hand. In the school tuck shop, this would buy me two boiled sweets. Once a week, I would further supplement this allowance from her handbag, and treat myself to an iced lolly stick for twenty-five paise. Or, if I was really lucky, a one-rupee coin would buy me a bottle of Double Seven Cola, or a slim bar of Cadbury's Milk Chocolate, wrapped in gold, and again in purple paper, and smelling of heaven. My brother Ramu, four years older, made purchases of a larger magnitude, and was considered by his friends to be a very lucky fellow.

This time my need was urgent. Sports Day was just two days

away, which meant an enticing array of snack stalls, just waiting for me to supply myself with spending money from my mother's purse. With my mother on the phone and her bag unattended, this was the chance I'd been waiting for.

Mary hid her surprise calmly. Her eyes held mine as her hand continued to explore the contents of the handbag. As I watched, she slowly pulled out two five-rupee notes from the bag. She glanced at them, and walked towards the door. Two days' salary, gained in twenty seconds.

I called her name.

What, she said. What missy, as though I have not seen you in here a hundred times, just like this.

I tried to block her path. "Put that money back," I said.

Move, she said.

"I'll tell my mother," I said.

Do that, she said, and you see what I will do. She pushed one of the notes into my hand. Here, keep this, she said. Keep quiet. If you tell your mother, Terrible Things will happen to you.

Mary tucked the other note into her saree blouse and walked away, leaving me staring at the five rupees she had put in my hand, more money than I had ever handled at one time.

My mother turned the corner just as Mary left the room. My hand slipped the five-rupee note into my pocket. My mother didn't see Mary. She walked into the bedroom and noticed the bag lying on the bed, the clasp undone. She stared at the bag, and then stared at me.

It took me five seconds to tell my mother that I had seen Mary stealing.

It took Mary half an hour. Crying, wailing, loosening her hair, beating her chest, telling my mother that she was innocent, but if my mother had any doubts to please search her, and if after that, there were still any doubts, to please take the money from her salary, for though she was innocent, she would gladly cut her entire salary to please my mother. Why, if my mother wished, she could cut Mary's hands off, and Mary would not mind. She was only there to serve. And all the while, her eyes never leaving me.

Half an hour to convince my mother of her innocence.

My mother was never a conscientious accountant, and couldn't tell exactly how much was missing. And the next morning, my school shirt was stained brown by the iron, my regulation white underwear was inexplicably torn, and my school shoes were left unpolished.

I wanted to complain to my mother, but her face that morning still carried traces of the upset of the evening before. So I said nothing. I looked hurriedly for a new shirt, changed into colored underwear, and desperately rubbed a piece of chalk over my white Keds to disguise the dirt. I was late to breakfast.

I was late to school.

I believed in Jesus.

It was difficult not to, given what the teachers said. Damnation and all. And I wasn't the only one, either. By the time I was in middle school, almost everyone I knew abandoned, for eight hours, the ganeshas and allahs and mahaveers and zoroasters that peopled our homes, to clad ourselves in a uniform designed for a much colder, straitlaced climate, and cheerfully (emblazered, en-tied) congregate in the school chapel first thing in the morning to watch a Senior Prefect step behind the lectern to chant ThisMorning'sLesson is from Proverbs, chapter thirty-one, verses ten to thirty-one, and then read out, heathen voice bell-like in the wood-paneled chapel, Who can find a virtuous woman For her price is far above rubies.

And as we learned to cross ourselves, thus, with the tips of our fingers: forehead to clavicle, left to right (no, idiot, not right to left), we were worried not by our rampant infidelness, but rather by the doubt: were we, in spite of all our efforts, really English enough?

We straightened our blazers

tightened our ties

and took comfort in the notion that so too did all our favorite characters—in the Gospel according to Enid Blyton.

For hers was the Power and the Glory, and all of us knew it. St. Enid, the true Messiah, who wrote of the frozen-in-time nineteen forties English childhood that we aspired to and were perpetually excluded from. We ate her alive. Swallowed her down. And the teachers in class may have droned on about the greatness of Indian culture (This Morning's Lesson: the history of India, volume two, chapter eight), but we always knew that, given a choice, we would:

study in Malory Towers and St. Clare's,

spend our holidays as part of the Famous Five, the Five Find-Outers, and the Secret Seven,

and have romantic, outlandish names like Jane.

With scorched shirt tucked carefully inside my pinafore, I kept my eyes on the chapel lectern and tried to look like I was paying attention. Every now and then, like a searchlight in a prison camp, I felt Mrs. Rafter's gaze sweep over me. After chapel, I was among those who had to stay behind to be scolded by the house captains (two points lost for coming late, one for unpolished shoes. And later, five more for wearing the wrong underwear) while the rest of the school filed out quietly. Tara tried to catch my eye meaningfully, and I smiled inquiringly back.

I didn't know she had sent me a note.

She didn't know I hadn't received it.

Mrs. Rafter was Anglo-Indian, like half the teachers in the school, but she pretended to be English. By our conservative estimate, she was at least as old as the school. She dyed what was left of her gray hair brown, hid the liver spots on her face with a dusty powder several shades paler than her skin, and stained her lips with pink lipstick. She wore shapeless dresses in floral patterns and plastic Bata slippers. She ate spicy fish sandwiches for lunch and perfumed her classes with her breath. She talked of her English grandfather, forbearing to recognize that he had slept with a village woman in the hills of Kemmanagundi to produce her mother. She was supposed to teach us Home Science, or how to be good wives and mothers, but actually it was her mission in life to mold the girls under her charge into little ladies. She taught us Deportment, and labored to correct the myriad regional accents in her classes: Sn-acks, children, not snakes. Raylways, not rilevays. She made her point with a long wooden ruler. Rilevays received one stroke on the palm. A chatty vaat yaar? in casual conversation, two.

When the Queen of England finally recognized her efforts on

behalf of English Culture and invited her to tea, Mrs. Rafter would have nothing to be ashamed of.

Our parents kept out of her way, and agreed with everything she said. It was hard not to. Who could object to her high moral standards? And certainly, a convent-educated accent was an asset. It would give the girls better marriage options. Most of all, they agreed with Mrs. Rafter's view that girls must be Good. It dovetailed nicely with their own notions of the fitness of things.

As in, Boys Will Be Boys,

but Girls Must Be Good.

This involved, primarily, keeping our knees together, and our minds pure. Pure, as in virginal. Innocent of the depredations of Man (or Boy), at least until their parental duty was done. Delivered, one girl, unsullied, to the marital bed. Her price far above rubies.

When Mrs. Rafter walked onto the sports field, we already knew that she was in a bad mood. Forty minutes of Mrs. Rafter's class first thing in the morning had resulted in:

Two copybooks flung out of the window for untidy writing.

Two girls punished with her ruler: on the legs to keep their knees together, on the arm to keep their backs from touching the chair. You creatures, she said, will never be Ladies. Why are you crying? You think good marks excuse bad behavior? Write one hundred times: I will learn to act like a Lady.

Sports Day practice sessions had intensified every day. Now, just two days before the big event, we did nothing else. The whole school spent hours out on the big field, practicing, training, running, jumping. The three school houses would be competing head-to-head, winning and losing points with every event. This was the only time of the year when the School Goddesses, the older girls, the House Captains, the Prefects, the School Captain, who chatted with such ease and familiarity with the teachers, would condescend to notice us, the junior girls. "Good jump!" they would call. "Well done," and we would look to see if our friends had noticed.

We practiced everything, including the cheers. We were divided into three houses, each named after the first school principals. On Sports Day we'd take turns shouting, house by house:

Two Four Six EIGHT,
Who do we appreciATE? . . . Kensington!
Whisky soda ginger POP,
Here comes Ashley . . . on the TOP!
North South East WEST,
Who is the Very BEST? . . . Brunton!

I was competing in the fifty-meter dash. Usually I was part of the scaff-and-raff, the greater lumpen herd, never one of those who won points at school by being good at studies, or who mastered the art of talking chirpily to the teachers and about whom they told parents, "Oh, she's *such* a nice girl!"; not losing house points was the best I could strive for. Luckily, a lifetime of being chased around my home by my older brother had given me a turn for speed that was unmatched. Winning the race meant winning fifty points for the house and smiles from the seniors and teachers. That one day on the sports field made up for my shabby academics and everything else.

That one day, I would shed the Sports Day skirt that modestly covered the Sports Day shorts below. I would race down the field ahead of everyone else, my braids flailing behind me, the house ribbon fluttering on my arm.

And when I did, for just a few minutes, my entire house, senior to junior, would chant in unison: Two-Four-Six-Eight-Who-Do-We-Appreciate?

Me.

I had just finished my practice run ("well done!") and had rejoined the rest of my class on the side of the field, when Mrs. Rafter appeared. I didn't care; teachers often came to watch us practice. I was more concerned with what my friends and I were going to do.

Usually, at practice sessions we hung around the older girls. As temperatures soared, they would casually remove their blazers and look over their shoulders. That was our signal to compete for the honor of holding their blazers, which also gave us the right to talk about it for a whole day afterwards. Not this year, though. This year, the four of us were absorbed in our own private club, which had started a few weeks earlier during lunchtime.

This was the most exciting club I had ever known. It was also the most secretive. It had just four members, Tara "Tash" Srinivasan, Freny "Bats" Batlivala, Susan "Benjy" Benjamin, and myself. And we all knew the penalty of getting caught.

I had just caught Tash's eye, and started waving in her direction, when I saw her eyes glaze over. I looked around, and knew right away that I was in for it.

Mrs. Rafter had come to a halt in front of my class. She had her ruler out. Today of all days, she was going to do a Surprise Check.

"Okay, girls," she said, and we all squatted to the floor in a straight line, knees apart. From where she stood, it gave her a straight view down our parted skirts right down to our underpants. They were supposed to be white. I, thanks to Mary, was wearing pink. Mrs. Rafter's voice silenced the entire great big field, and all the girls on it.

You girl!

Yes, you.

Stand up.

What is that rubbish you are wearing?

Come here.

The ruler in her hand lifted the edge of my skirt high enough for everyone to see.

Look at this, she said. Decent girls wear white, my girl. Doesn't your mother know that?

Answer me, girl.

Do you have a tongue in your head or is it completely empty?

My classmates, from the safety of white underpants, giggled dutifully.

Hold out your hand, girl.

Why are you crying?

I hated Mary. As soon as I got home, I was going to climb onto the terrace, go to my special hiding place, unearth that five-rupee note that she had given me, and go show it to my mother, and tell her the truth. Then, I would show her my pink underwear, and the red mark of Mrs. Rafter's ruler that always took hours to fade.

Then, Mary would see.

My friends led me away to one corner of the field, and waited impatiently for me to finish crying.

"Are we having a club meeting?" I asked, drying my tears.

"Yes, of course we are," said Tash. "Didn't you get my note?"

No, I said.

"Well, doesn't matter. It probably fell on the floor and got lost."

Supposing someone finds it, I asked, my hand still smarting. "Don't worry," said Tash. "Nobody will find it."

"Okay, here's the story," she said. "It's a Famous Five one."

Oh goody, we said, and made sure that no one was close to us, listening.

"Julian, Dick and George and Ann are driving along in the car to a picnic."

What color was the car? we asked. And what were they wearing?

"The car was . . . okay, blue. And they weren't wearing anything. They were Naked."

I went home that evening, eager to talk to my mother about Mary.

I never got the chance.

I was met by my mother, who didn't smile, who didn't hug me, or ask me how Sports Day practice went.

"Explain this," she said, holding out a five-rupee note.

"I found this in your desk drawer," she said.

No, I wanted to say. You could not have. I had hidden it up on the terrace the previous evening, in a hiding place I thought only I knew. A little niche, hidden by brickwork. Big enough for small secrets.

Except I should have remembered that, years ago, it was Mary who had first shown it to me.

Later, I heard my mother crying to my father: "I forced her to apologize to Mary. Bad girl. So shocking. We have never had trouble like this with Ramu. Yes, of course I am going to punish her. I was going to make puri-palya for her lunch tomorrow, but now I won't."

I stayed awake for a long time that night. I waited for my parents to go to sleep, before slipping from my bed and running into the drawing room. I still had one more thing to do that day, for our club meeting.

Tomorrow was my turn, and I wanted to outdo them all. I couldn't make up stories the way Tash did, but alternatives were acceptable. They were just more dangerous.

The drawing room was lined with books. I switched on the torch and spelled my way through the titles, until I came to the one I wanted. "Harold Robbins," it said. It was on the Forbidden shelf, banned not just to me but to my brother Ramu as well. But of course he had read every book on that shelf, and from things he had said, I knew that this was the book I wanted. I was slipping it off the shelf when I heard her voice, clothed in darkness:

Oho, missy. And what would your mother say if she saw you now?

I ran.

Ran back to my room, and threw the book under the bed.

And waited for Mary to follow.

She didn't, and the house grew quiet. After a while, I rescued the book and tucked it into the bottom of my schoolbag. I went to sleep.

But the next day, in school, when I triumphantly gathered my club members around me, the book was missing.

Our club had started, as most school stuff did, during lunch break.

Lunchtime in school was fifteen minutes of urgent swallowing, followed by half an hour of play. When we were ten, we would take our lunch boxes to a far corner of the big field and have a picnic. Lunch was usually sandwiches: cucumber, coconut-and-mint chutney, cheese, or jam, packed into plastic lunch boxes that had a separate compartment for chips or biscuits. Sometimes our mothers would provide roti rolls instead: chapatis with cooked vegetables rolled up inside, or jam, or spicy mango pickle. The four of us would trade bites, everyone else's lunch always tasting better than our own, and fantasize about the meals we would really like to have. Naturally, all our secret food fantasies revolved around English food, exotic fare that

Enid Blyton said tasted better than anything else in the world. Steak and kidney pie. Roast beef. Ham and watercress sandwiches.

And then we'd walk round and round the field, and talk endlessly, about our classmates, our families, and when we would get our menstrual periods, in the manner of girls who are just discovering the art of female conversation.

It was Tash, naturally enough, who escalated the thing to a whole new level. She announced impressively one day: "Yesterday I had sex."

Sandwiches were forgotten. Really? Why yes, she said. Really. Just yesterday, she and Phiroze, a ten-year-old boy who lived next door, went behind his house, took off their clothes, and Had Sex. Were you sitting or standing, we asked. Tash thought it through for a minute and said, Standing. That's how it's always done. And then, to seal her expertise, she used the Word: we Fucked, she said, and watched as Bats, Benjy, and I rolled about on the ground, squealing and giggling.

We knew the basic theory, of course: we had all pored through the *Reader's Digest Family Health Guide* (available in every home), staring in silence at the picture of the naked woman (eighteen years old, according to the caption), and wondering if the senior girls in our school indeed had breasts like that, and waists like that, and god forbid, hair all over their privates. Then we'd turn the page over to the picture of the man (naked, also at eighteen years) and have a collective fit of the giggles. The guide described sex as "the insertion of the penis into the vagina," but we knew better: sex was when a man's su-su and a woman's su-su touched.

But according to Tash, we really knew nothing at all.

Her authority was unchallenged. She'd come up with new stories, some to do with herself, others to do with our favorite storybook characters, who were always naked, and who had sex, it appeared, with hundreds of people, and all at the same time. We would listen agog, our heads close together, our feet walking, walking, round and round the field. We listened during lunchtime, we whispered in chapel, we waited for sports practice. We knew for certain that if we were ever caught, we would be severely punished. Maybe even expelled. "That's why," said Tash, "we have to meet Far From Everybody."

Accordingly, we called ourselves the Far From Everybody Club, and we waited for Tash's creative genius to send us a note: FFEC meeting. Field. Lunchtime. That meant she'd thought of another good one. After a while, Tash got tired and we all had to take turns and come up with something new.

That day was my turn, but somebody had abstracted the Harold Robbins from my bag. I fretted furiously. Was it someone at school? Or was it Mary at home?

I didn't know which was worse.

"Never mind the book," said Tash. "Tell us a story. Yourself and somebody else."

My brain struggled to come up with something, but it was difficult. I couldn't make up anything. The only thing I could possibly tell them about myself and somebody else wasn't some silly make-believe. It happened to be true.

But the truth was the one thing I couldn't really talk about. Not to my mother. Not to my friends. Truth was either like the *Reader's Digest* or like my secret. Boring, or shameful.

* * *

When I was little and disobeyed Mary or threw a tantrum, she was not allowed to smack me. That was a privilege reserved for my mother alone. Instead, she would devise new and interesting ways to keep me quiet. She slipped me forbidden sweets. She threw away the milk I did not want to drink and told my mother I had drunk it all. Sometimes she would drink it herself.

By the time I was four, Mary had learned to manage me as she did my mother. Sometimes, though, I would still disobey her and run to hide behind my mother. Who would either scold me or scold Mary, depending on her mood. Like all baby-ayahs, Mary learned to cope with the magic rule: all credit for good behavior was given to me; any problems were attributed to Mary directly. "Not drunk her milk? Why? Why are you letting her behave like this?" my mother would ask. "What happened, baby? Mary scolded you and made you cry? Don't scold her. Just tell her. She will listen, she is a good little *gundu*."

And Mary would agree with her, and nod her head in appreciation, and smile at me, and I, victorious, would put my hand in hers, while my mother watched in a pleased, self-satisfied way. See? she seemed to say. Any problems, just come to me.

Except, that is, when she was resting, or in the midst of preparing to go out. Then my mother's temper would boil over.

One day, I had fussed and fussed. Mary had already drunk the milk I hated, winning me a distracted "good girl!" from my mother. Mary had handed me two sweets, which I greedily consumed, one after another. And still I fussed. My mother shouted, first at me, then at Mary. She needed to leave for a lunch party, she was late, and I was clinging fussily to her saree, refusing to let her go.

So Mary took me into the bathroom, raised my frock, removed my underpants, and made me lie down on the floor.

Don't tell your mother, she said, and rubbed the palm of her hand between my legs.

I didn't tell my friends that story, that day out on the field.

We talked of other things. I told everybody, for the hundredth time, how I would be going to England that summer for the holidays, and how, since they were my best friends, I would bring them back a piece of English pie.

But of course, I didn't go that summer. It was another three years before I went, and was finally able to sit down in a restaurant and order steak and kidney pie. Don't, said the adults at the table. You won't like it. I will *love* it, I replied. Just as Julian and Dick and Pip and Bets loved it. And then the dish arrived, and I breathed in, nose quivering in disbelief, the reek of urine mingled with the fetid smell of beef. I bolted. Fifty meters to the bathroom, braids flailing behind me, hand over my mouth.

But that day, out on the field, I still fantasized. Look, I said, pulling the chapati and vegetable roll out of my lunch box. Meat pie. We all laughed, and everybody pretended that their lunch was something different too.

Roast beef.

Sausage rolls.

Liver and onions.

And then we wandered back to class, still laughing, still planning the next club meeting. Tomorrow was Sports Day, no time then. Perhaps on Monday.

* * *

Mrs. Rafter was waiting for me.

Somebody had left Tash's note to me on her table. I never did find out who. It said:

"F F E Club meeting today. Sports field. Your turn tomorrow to tell story about Bets, Daisy, and naked boys. Or bring something to show."

Tash, prudently, hadn't signed her name to it. But right on top, after folding it, she had written mine.

Mrs. Rafter broke a ruler on my hand that day.

She read the note out to the whole class, so everyone would know.

She made a phone call to my mother, who came to pick me up.

And though I cried, I never once told Mrs. Rafter who the other club members were. Members of the Famous Five and Secret Seven would never squeal on their friends, I knew.

If Enid Blyton were to ever rise up from her grave and invite me to tea, I would have nothing to be ashamed of.

My mother said nothing to me on the way home. Perhaps she had already decided to let my father handle this. This was not just acting rude to the servants. Or complaining of the food she served. This was even worse than petty larceny, though that was bad enough.

This crossed over into the realm of Dangerous Thoughts that had no place in Girls from Good Families. This was Chi-Chi.

That morning, in chapel, a visiting evangelist named James Jacob had told us amusing stories from the Bible and the fate (Dire Doom) that awaited little girls who did not take Jesus to their Hearts. I wasn't too sure what he meant by Doom, but when he asked if you love Jesus raise your hand, I, along with everyone else, did. He must have seen the temporary, school-bound nature of my interest, however, because I went straight to Doom, and Satan, in the shape of Mary, was waiting there for me.

My father returned home that evening, and was listening to my mother's horrified tale when Mary walked slowly into the room. Her head was bent. When she spoke, her voice was so low.

Oh, Ma, Mary said. Oh, Ma.

See what I found under missy's bed.

And as she held out the Harold Robbins book with shaking hand, tears rolled down her cheeks.

My mother took the book. Mary didn't leave. Squatting down next to my mother, she began whispering. And my mother, listening, began to cry.

Oh, Ma. There's more. Terrible thing she is doing, Ma, which, god willing, only you can correct. Through your goodness, Ma. But please excuse what I am about to say. Forgive me.

I am seeing her in the bathroom, Ma. She is doing chi-chi things to herself.

Chi-chi Mary.

Chi-chi Me.

Four years old, and for months afterwards, I quietened magically, riveted by the sensations Mary's hand evoked between my legs.

It was our secret, she said. Don't tell your mother.

If you do, Terrible Things will happen to you.

I think the massages between my legs stopped when I became, in a couple of years, a little too old to listen to Mary. But by the time I was ten, I knew I should have told my mother about them, even if what Mary said was true: your mother will never believe you, missy. She will think you are a naughty, disgusting little girl for telling such lies.

I should have told my mother. I was a bad girl for not doing so.

And I was bad when, recently, bouncing up and down in the swimming pool, I felt the same chi-chi sensations blooming below my waist. And blooming afresh in the bathroom, when I tried to emulate the movement of Mary's hands between my legs all those years ago.

Bad.

Shameful.

Chi-chi.

I knew I deserved the punishment that my father meted out to me that day: when the family went to England that summer, I would not go with them. I would stay with my grandmother instead.

And: I was not to participate in Sports Day. Silver cups and medals were meant for Good Girls.

And: That evening, I would not join the family on their dinner outing. I would stay at home and think about the wrong I had done.

No one could ever marry me, and I was destined to bring even more shame on my parents' heads.

Two four six eight
Indian girls don't masturbate

I watched my family leave for dinner. The cook took the evening off to go to a movie. Mary and I were left alone in the house.

Whisky soda ginger pop
Knees together hands on top

Every evening, Mary climbed the steel ladder to the roof, to collect the clothes that had been drying on the clothesline. She would roll the dry clothes into a bundle and, carrying it carefully in one hand, would feel her way down the ladder with her feet. It was a simple affair: two poles of steel, with holes at frequent intervals to hold the rungs, tightened into place by screws. I had climbed that ladder a million times on my way to the roof and knew it well.

That evening, I followed Mary to the terrace. I waited until she was busy with the clothes, before removing three rungs set fairly high up on the ladder, one right after the other. She would not see them missing, I knew. Her feet would feel for them routinely, already lowering her weight onto them, before she realized the futility of doing so. Her arms would be of no use to her, I knew. They would be too full of clothes. And I would stand back at that moment, and watch her foot slip into the lightness of air, and I would watch the weight of her body tumble, like a bird with wings of sunbaked clothes. And I would watch her land, and the clothes settle lightly about her, and I would watch the clothes turn red, then brown, as they dried once more.

And I would replace the rungs, and nobody would ever know.

*   *   *

I waited in the shadows, beneath that ladder, listening to Mary approach. Some instinct stopped her; she called out from the edge of the terrace:

Put them back, missy, or I will create even more trouble for you.

That's when I stepped out and said: "Go ahead."

And perhaps she finally saw the newfound strength in my eyes that day, staring up at her, but she never bothered me again. She stayed with my mother for another fifteen years, a silent figure in the background; silent, wretched, underpaid; careful and polite around me, still obsequious around my mother.

I didn't care. School was still the place that mattered. Five years later, I became Games Captain and a School Prefect, and Mrs. Rafter laid a heavy hand about my shoulder. "Well *done*, my girl," she said, her potent breath wheezing into my face. "I always knew you could do it. One of our best girls," she would tell visiting parents.

And I would straighten my blazer and smile politely, ignoring the younger girls who clustered eagerly around.

THE RED CARPET

Rangappa was content to live in a realm of different names. Officially, as per his one-page bio-data, prepared for a small sum by one of the roadside typists who serviced the lawyers outside Bangalore's Mayo Hall, his name was T. R. Gavirangappa.

Tharikere Ranganatha Gavirangappa. Anyone reading his name would instantly know that he hailed from the village of Tharikere, near the hills of Chikmagalur, and that he was the son of Ranganatha. His family called him Rangappa for short.

But at work he was known as Raju.

This nominal transformation was announced to him, quite casually, at the end of his job interview.

"Your driving test was satisfactory," his prospective employer said. "The job is yours, provided you are courteous, prompt, and steady in your habits." And then: "Oh, and on the job, you will be called Raju."

It had not really occurred to him to protest, so everyone in the house, from the cook to his employer's little three-year-old daughter, called him Raju. It had taken him three days to get used to it. And, after a while, he had even begun to like it. There was a film star called Raju. It was that kind of name: snappy, spry, a certain air about it. After many months on the job he suggested to his family that perhaps they too should consider calling him Raju, but his father laughed at him and that was that.

He had heard about the job from his cousin, who worked as an office boy and whose boss needed a driver for his family. It would not be a company job, unfortunately—those were the best kind, with all sorts of perks and bonuses and (best of all) membership to a union that prevented you from getting fired easily. Instead, he would be hired directly by the boss's family; but they were good people, his cousin said, and would pay well. Raju (or Rangappa) heard this out with a sense of reserve; if he got the job, his cousin would be sure to earn a tip, and the promise of that was bound to make *any* boss look good.

He was to go interview immediately with the boss's wife, a Mrs. Choudhary.

His heart sank at the news. His father, also a driver, had once worked for a Mrs. Choudhary. He had taken the young Rangappa (or Raju) to see her, hoping to receive a gift for his son— some money, perhaps, or even a packet of biscuits. Rangappa remembered standing with his father on the steps of a large house, not daring to sit, waiting for Mrs. Choudhary to emerge for her ritual round of morning shopping. He remembered a formidable woman, clad in silks and jewelry and with a round red *bindi* on her forehead so large it seemed to swallow him up. His father presented him; she ignored him and told his father to hurry up with the car. Rangappa-soon-to-be-Raju had never been more scared in his life.

He wished he could turn his cousin down. He decided he didn't like the sound of the job (the other Mrs. Choudhary's voice resonating frighteningly through the years), and besides, he didn't really want to be beholden to his cousin, whom he suspected of harboring evil designs on his younger sister. Far better to say no: to his cousin, to this Mrs. Choudhary. Far better, indeed, to spend his time on getting his younger sister married off and safe.

But he didn't have a choice. His salary had to support his parents, his sister, his wife of four years, and their baby daughter. The driving job he had right now paid enough to feed any two of them, after deducting his daily bus fare to and from work. They were all always a little hungry. This new job, this Mrs. Choudhary job, offered much more—at least, according to his cousin.

He woke up early on the morning of the interview, rushing to fetch two buckets of water for his house from the pump down the road. He hastily washed his face and hands before joining his family for morning prayers in front of the *pooja* altar, manufactured by placing the colored portraits of various deities on a shelf and decorating them with flowers, turmeric and red kumkum powders, and a bit of green velvet with gold trim. The smoky fragrance of the incense sticks filtered through his senses. He chanted the Sanskrit verses for the spiritual welfare of his family and the good of the world along with his father, but his mind charted an alternate course of prayer: for this new job, and a little bit of money.

Afterwards, he stood in front of a mirror that hung lopsided on one cracked and peeling wall. He felt sticky and tired from the heat of the night, but the water shortage in the district prevented him from having a bath. Two buckets of water would have to wash and feed his family for that entire day. He took a little coconut oil from his wife's bottle and rubbed it into his hair before combing it neatly through.

"You should take a bath," his father said, from the stoop in front of the house. He had sat there every morning since his injured back had forced his retirement, sipping his morning tumbler of coffee. "And, very important, you need a new, clean shirt. Otherwise they won't hire you. You should look smart. I know these things. Daughter, give your husband a new shirt."

Rangappa's wife looked timidly at him. He had no new shirt, hadn't had one for a while. "There is no new shirt, Appa," Rangappa told his father. "Never mind. I'll go as I am."

"Well, don't blame me if you don't get the job. I know about these things. If you come back empty-handed, don't blame me."

The Choudhary house stood in a large garden, two stories high and gleaming whitely at the end of a cement driveway edged with rosebushes whose blossoms would never be plucked for the altar but would remain in the garden to wither and die at their master's pleasure. Rangappa's first glimpse of the house didn't reduce the tension in his back. He knew that the obvious wealth of his prospective employers didn't automatically translate into better working conditions. Some of these memsahibs could fight over the last rupee with all the possessive fierceness of those old crones who sold vegetables in the early morning market.

The watchman at the gate escorted him to the front door, surrendering him to the maid who answered. She asked him to leave his shoes at the door and step into the foyer. "Wait here. I'll tell her you've come."

Rangappa studied the maid carefully. She looked well fed. She wore a saree that he would have loved to buy for his wife. She didn't seem cowed or rude. These were good signs.

"Who is it?" A woman's lazy voice came from the landing of the curving staircase in the corner and Rangappa looked up. He felt himself seized by shock. He stared at the apparition for a quick instant, and immediately looked down at the floor in embarrassment. The voice said: "Someone for the driver job? Oh, good. Ask him to wait, I'll be right down."

Rangappa's thoughts held him paralyzed in disbelief. He couldn't reconcile the bizarre figure he had witnessed with the haughty memsahib of his imaginings. That slip of a girl, no older than his teenage sister surely, was practically *naked:* wearing nothing more than a man's banian vest and a pair of loose shorts that, together, exposed most of her legs, all of her arms, and a good bit of her chest. The maid didn't seem to be bothered by this, and Rangappa immediately worried: what manner of a house was this?

He was a decent, respectable man.

The marble floor beneath his feet ran in every direction, giving way, here and there, to carpets that glowed with the jewel-bright colors of a silken wedding saree. Rangappa's eye traced the dull gleam on the heavy bronze sculptures, which, along with the sofas and the paintings and the dark wooden cabinets rich with objects that glistened and shone, reminded him of a movie set. But instead of stepping away at the end of a day's shooting, these people lived on, in their movie-star lives.

Except, from what he had seen, this set seemed to lack a proper heroine.

The next time Mrs. Choudhary appeared, she had aged about a decade and a half. Gone was that young sprightliness, vanished behind a thick robe that stretched from shoulder to ankles and belted at her waist. She seated herself on a sofa and asked the maid to bring her some coffee. Her voice was soft and polite, but Raju had seen memsahibs with soft and polite voices turn into screaming banshees when faced with a minor transgression. He stood alert. She sipped her coffee and studied his résumé, which he'd presented to her in a tattered envelope: a single sheet of paper, folded and refolded, marked with brown creases, smudged with fingerprints, and with the words BIO-DATA typed at the top of the page in large capital letters.

When describing it all later to his father, he portrayed his role in the interview with a savoir faire he'd never really felt, and omitted to mention how his hands had left the steering wheel of the car sticky with perspiration during the driving test. He did talk about how she'd made him drive right into the worst traffic the city had to offer, and had praised the way he'd handled it. He talked of her commandments, completely contrary to the prevalent conventional wisdom on the crazy, unruly city roads: when driving for her, he was to drive slowly and, oddly, to follow the rules, follow the rules, follow the rules.

Back at her house after the driving test, she resumed her seat on the sofa, her face set in stern lines behind her glasses. His relief at her praise instantly abated. Now began the inevitable battle over his qualifications and his salary, between his need and her whimsy. And, by the looks of her, she would not be a pushover.

"Your driving test was satisfactory," she said. "The job is yours, provided you are courteous, prompt, and steady in your habits."

He waited. He hadn't mentioned his expectations, wanting to hear what she would offer first. Then, if it was too low, perhaps no more than what he was currently earning, he would try bargaining, begging, pleading. He would tell her of his family's poverty and the many mouths that needed to be fed. Not that it would work, necessarily; memsahibs always treated such stories as just that—stories, tales that their domestic staff conjured up out of the air for a momentary amusement. He waited.

She nodded briskly and named a salary that was two and a half times what he was making. In his elation he forgot all about the first rule in a wage negotiation: keep an impassive face, and hold out for more. He grinned happily, and barely heard what she said next:

"Oh, and on the job, you will be called Raju."

At home, later, he handed around celebratory sweetmeats and recounted to his family how he was then told to go around to the kitchen; how the cook, Julie, an immense woman (obviously a devoted servant of her own art), had introduced him to the other servants in the house: Shanti, the baby-ayah, who'd opened the door to him that morning; Thanga, the top-work maid, who cleaned the house; and Gowda, the silent little gardening boy. How she had given him hot, sweet tea and a freshly made rava dosa, the semolina batter mixed with onions and green chilies and fried thin and crisp and delicious. And how she had told him that as long as he worked there, all his meals would be catered for from that large kitchen, as per the memsahib's orders. Breakfast when he arrived, lunch at one, tea or coffee on demand.

Rangappa-now-Raju did some boasting that day. He never did share that extraordinary first moment, though, when his employer had cavorted into his presence in the most indecent of clothes, like one of those scandalous females on the foreign TV channels. He never mentioned that. And a full week passed before he told his family of the change in his professional name.

And so he settled down to working for Mrs. Choudhary. Of course, he didn't call her that. When he first started work, he'd refer to her as "Amma," but soon found that even that wasn't quite suitable. The other servants in the house called her Madam, pronounced not as the word's English originators had imagined but rather "May-dum." As in "May-dum *kareethidhare*"—Madam wants you. "May-dum *oota maduthidhare*"— Madam is eating her lunch.

His routine remained unchanged through the first year. He'd arrive by eight, catching two buses to do so, and straightaway wash and polish both the cars, hoping to finish in time to grab a quick cup of coffee before driving May-dum's little daughter and her ayah to school. He always finished cleaning the big black car first. It was one of the latest brands, and May-dum's husband, the Saibru, drove it himself, jealously refusing to let anyone else touch the wheel. Raju always had it clean and ready for the Saibru when he exited the house at 8:30 in a hurry. Raju would salute him and receive a nod for his pains; the two men hadn't exchanged more than a dozen words to date.

Then he'd clean her car, which was just as smart. Even smarter, Raju thought, loving its gleaming whiteness and fancy interior. He was aware that she didn't share his opinion on this. The car had arrived from the showroom about six months after he'd joined. He had inspected it with extreme pride and possessiveness. This was *his* car, really—the one that he would drive, the one that he'd be seen driving. It was a prestigious make. He had peeped inside at the opulent furnishings: the velvet seats, the rich tone of the red carpet. His fingers itched to take the wheel.

She's going to love this, he thought.

She didn't. She came out to inspect it with a girlfriend, and her first comment was "Oh god, not white!"

Raju threw the door open for her inspection and immediately she groaned. "Will you look at this, Anu? Velvet seats! Oh god, and that red carpet! Could anything be in worse taste?"

Her friend, Miss Anasuya, considered the matter and said, "Well, at least the windows aren't tinted black."

"That's true." May-dum laughed. "Then it would definitely look like a greasy politician's car!"

"Oh, it still does," said her friend.

Whatever their opinion, Raju still felt proud of the car. He just wished his family could see him driving it.

Some time passed before he realized that there was more to this job than just driving a car. His father had been right, after all.

"You must act smart," the old man had said. "You don't know how to act smart. You are going to lose this good job because you must act smart and not like a coolie. When that happens, don't blame me."

At first he'd ignored his father, especially when he'd carry on about how to open the car door ("Open the door, hold it open while she gets in or out, and then close it firmly but not loudly"), demonstrating on an imaginary car handle and clutching his aching back all the while. And then one day it dawned on Raju that perhaps his father was right. Previously, Raju had worked as a transport driver for small manufacturing companies that used little minivans to transport goods and people. Cost and speed were of the essence there; the niceties of life didn't really matter. But now he was in a different sphere. He started to pay attention to how other drivers did things, at the big hotels, or at the Club, where May-dum liked to meet her friends. It was true. The smartest drivers acted so. One evening he really listened to his father's lecture, in the surprise of which the old gentleman enthusiastically lengthened his words by a half hour, and got up to demonstrate so often that his back suffered for it the whole night long.

The next morning, Raju was ready.

As soon as May-dum appeared, he leaped to open the door, standing (smartly, he hoped) to attention. She paused, surprise and amusement warring on her face, and then she smiled. "Thank you," she said, and slid into the car. The warmth of that smile stayed with him the entire day.

From his father he learned to greet her cheerily the first thing every morning. He bought a can of air freshener with his own money, and, as he'd seen another driver in the Club do, he'd spray the car interiors with it before driving from the car park to the main clubhouse to pick her up. He learned to anticipate her movements, running to carry her bags as soon as she emerged from the shops, staying alert for the sudden sound of her voice. Watchful to see which side of the car she approached, so that he could have the car door open and ready for her. After a while, he learned to tell, just by looking at her dress, whether she wanted to visit the gym, go shopping, or meet with her friends. Sometimes, he could even guess correctly what music she would play on the car stereo.

And in return, she never raised her voice at him.

No screaming at him when the car got stuck in traffic. No shouting that he was a fool, and the son of fools. No muttering that he should be fired, the idiot, the rascal, just let him try and get another job as good as this.

That was the nicest thing about her; nicer in a way than even the wages, or the good meals, or even her carelessly handed-over parcels of food and old but still excellent clothing that made her especially interesting to his family. She never raised her voice. She was always polite. Raju's father would shake his head slowly when he heard that. "That's rare," he would say. "Very rare. Son, don't be stupid and lose this job and allow your family to starve. Take my advice. You won't get such a place again easily."

She didn't shout even when things went wrong, when, for instance, he dented the side of the new car by backing into a truck that wasn't supposed to be there. That was a moment when, he felt, she was fully entitled to lose her temper and lecture him angrily. Instead, she just went over the incident with him in detail, accepted his fervent apologies, and asked him to ensure that it never happened again.

The other servants in the house seemed to be aware of this as well. In a mixture of fashion and harsh reality, it was routine for domestic workers to complain to each other about their work conditions: the rotten food, the meager salaries, the unsympathetic memsahibs; at times it seemed almost a competition on who had it worse. The staff here never did that. Certainly, when eating together and gossiping, they traded hard-luck stories. That was only to be expected, for who did not have sorrow in their lives? But then, they would also tell him: "You know, if you have any problems, you should talk to May-dum about it. She'll help."

But in those early days he couldn't see himself taking the liberty. Besides, just the previous day, for the first time in years, he had bought a chicken on the way home from work, and the rare sweetness of the meat still flowed in his veins, mellowing his view of the world.

After a while he gave up trying to resolve the inherent contradiction in May-dum: that someone who made such an ideal employer—who, indeed, redefined his very notion of memsahibs—could also, simultaneously, present what he could characterize as nothing other than a Lax Moral Outlook. It wasn't just her style of dressing: scanty outfits that revealed her arms, her midriff, her legs in fashions most suitable for a prostitute or a film star or a foreigner. It was also her style of speaking with her friends: curses, jokes, comments, and conversation of a frankness that, on the whole, made him grateful that he could barely follow the English they spoke.

And then, she smoked. When Raju's younger brother had started smoking, their father had thrashed the living daylights out of him as soon as he found out about it. His brother still smoked, but was always careful to do it discreetly and never in front of the family elders. Not so his May-dum. She lit up casually, elaborately, luxuriously, all over the place, leaving a trail of noxious fumes behind her.

He was still very new when, one day, he'd driven her and one of her girlfriends out to lunch. She'd introduced him laughingly as her new driver, and he had smiled politely and touched his forehead at the friend. When they were both inside the car, he heard the friend comment: "Wasn't your last driver also called Raju?"

"Actually, his name was Murugesh."

"Hm. I could swear . . ." The other woman looked confused.

Raju knew all about this Murugesh-also-called-Raju. A competent driver, he'd been fired for drinking on the job. At first this had pleased Raju, as evidence of his employer's probity. But that was, of course, before he knew May-dum better. It was not the drink that she objected to; it was driving while drunk. He'd rapidly learned that firsthand.

Sometimes, on a Friday or Saturday, she'd ask him to stay late, past his six o'clock end-of-duty. She'd pay him extra for his overtime, and give him dinner, so it wasn't really a problem. His family liked the extra money. The first time, she'd gone out to a formal dinner, dressed in a saree and looking lovely.

The next time had been different: she was dressed, first of all, in a skirt so short that it couldn't have been longer than the span of his hand. Then she asked him to drive her to a pub. He knew all about such places: they were nothing more than elaborate versions of the drinking hells that dotted his own neighborhood, where men he'd known as boys had become dissolute and useless and a burden to their wives and families.

He had waited outside the pub for May-dum for four hours, watching the stream of fashionable, alien traffic enter a door from which music, lights, and the thin smell of alcohol emerged, until midnight had been and gone. Then he finally saw her again, clinging to the arm of another woman and laughing.

"Here's Raju! He'll drop us home."

He'd opened the door and stood there woodenly while the two women fumbled and crawled their way into the backseat. The enclosed car was filled with the fumes of their breath. They both smelled of smoke and dissipation. They'd laughed and giggled, out of control, all the way to their respective homes.

He knew: this behavior was unacceptable.

Immoral.

Should be stopped.

He also knew that he shouldn't, by any calculation, like and respect May-dum so much.

But there didn't seem to be anything he could do about that either.

This wasn't something he could discuss with any of his coworkers—the maids in the house seemed to have developed a strange blindness where May-dum was concerned, excusing behavior in her that they would have condemned in anyone else. And he could never bring himself to mention this aspect of her at home.

Really, the only person who seemed to criticize May-dum

was her mother-in-law—and that was another situation that bothered Raju a lot. A few months after he'd joined, Shanti came out one morning to ask him to have the car by the front door in ten minutes.

"She's going to visit her mother-in-law," she said. "The old lady is just back from a visit to her other son's house in America."

Her mother-in-law? Lives in the same city? Raju inquired in some surprise. Why do they not then live in the same house? This was unheard-of.

May-dum's face, when she emerged, was preoccupied. He studied it in the rearview mirror while he drove, as she stared out the window at the passing traffic, looking wistfully at cars moving in the opposite direction. They arrived very quickly at another large bungalow.

"Keep the car running and ready to leave," she told Raju before entering the house. He thought about it, and then decided that she must have been joking—there had been an odd note in her voice. He decided to wait where he was; if she was in a hurry, it wouldn't take him long to start the car. It was a good decision, because she finally reappeared a whole hour later.

With her, standing on the steps, was a diminutive woman whose voice carried all the way over to him. Was that her mother-in-law? Raju mechanically drove the car up to the steps of the house, opened the door for May-dum, took a set of bags from her and placed them inside the car, before turning to study her companion. He got a shock. The little lady standing next to her was the same Mrs. Choudhary who had terrorized him all those years ago. She was still dressed in silk and large bindis, her voice still had that harsh edge that repulsed, but sometime in the past fifteen years she had shrunk in size. Now, when had that happened?

As before, she ignored him. She was saying to May-dum: ". . . so wear the clothes I have bought for you. They will suit you more than that rubbish that you always wear. More proper. More suitable. And the frock for Baby is also very pretty, na? Much better than those shorts you put her in, poor thing. I always feel so bad when I look at her, dressed like that."

May-dum's smile didn't waver, at least until the car was on its way.

Raju glanced in the rearview mirror and saw her eyes filling with uncontrollable tears. And though Mother-in-law Choudhary's words expressed his sentiments exactly, at that moment, all he wanted to say was: please don't be upset by that woman— she's awful, I know, but she shrinks with time.

When they got home, she handed the bags to him. "There are some clothes in there," she said. "Perhaps your wife will like them. And take the dresses for your daughter."

He peeked inside the bag before protesting. He could see expensive sarees in bright colors, a child's frilly frock in pink. They were lovely, but already he knew that May-dum wouldn't think so. "But, May-dum, they are brand-new."

She smiled kindly at him. "Well, that's good, isn't it?"

Gradually, over the course of the first year, he stopped worrying about her inappropriate deportment and just accepted it as one of life's irregularities, just like that politician who seemed to have earned all the graces of god through corrupt, wicked living.

Didn't think about it, that is, until today.

Today he was once again concerned about her comportment. Feverishly, anxiously concerned. What would she wear?
Something decent, or not? He had a sudden mental image of her
appearing in scanty shorts, a cigarette in one hand and a bottle of
whisky in the other, and his heart almost failed. What if she did
dress like that? Then, he immediately resolved, he would just
have to pretend that he couldn't find the right directions; he had
lost his way, lost his mind, something like that.

He could never take her to meet his family if she was dressed
like that.

This momentous visit was the product of a conversation he'd
had with her about a month earlier. It had come about casually
enough. May-dum had been busy at her desk all morning, and
then handed him a set of bills, the cheque payments neatly attached, along with instructions on where each was to be paid.
The last item was her daughter's annual school fees, a large but
apparently appropriate amount for three hours of supervised
singing and paint-spattering every weekday.

"And what about your daughter, Raju?" she asked casually at
the end, raising the tip of her spectacles with one hand and rubbing her eyes with the other. "Are you sending her to school
somewhere?"

Raju nodded dumbly.

Of all the passions of his soul, one reigned supreme. He worshipped his little daughter. She had just turned three, but when
she was born, he could already envisage the successes of her life
as he held her tiny body in his hands. She would be educated. She
would be healthy and well nourished. She would be proud. Well

dressed. Beautiful. She would work in an office, in a job that would one day earn her a car of her own. She would be a may-dum in her own right.

His mother wanted to call the baby Kanthamma, after her own mother, but Raju said no. He'd already decided to call her Hema Malini, after the film actress, his first sight of whom (as a young boy) he had never forgotten: the most beautiful woman in the universe, a dream girl with liquid eyes and glowing skin and hair that tumbled down her back. His father told him it didn't matter what he named the baby. He commiserated: "Your first-born is a girl. That's a shame. My firstborn was a boy. A man should have three sons and a daughter, just like I did. That is glory. But don't worry. Next time you will have a boy. You are my son, after all."

Raju wasn't worried. He had thought the whole thing through quite a while back and, independent of his father, had made a few decisions. That night, after dinner, while lying next to his wife and listening to the heavy breathing of his parents sleeping in another corner of the same room, he told her his ideas: not having a son didn't matter; they would bring up their daughter to be strong and self-reliant. In fact, with the cost of living so high, perhaps they shouldn't try for another child, boy or girl, no matter what his father said. Better to have one child and look after her well than to have more and leave them half-starved. If money improved, then later, perhaps, they could reconsider. In the meantime, they had been visited by a little goddess and they were to be grateful. His wife was herself one of nine children, born into a family where daughters were considered the usual burden. If she was uncomfortable with Raju's odd ideas, she didn't comment.

After Raju got his current job, he was doubly convinced of the truth of his belief. Little Hema, with her tears and laughter and mischief, was none other than a manifestation of the Goddess Lakshmi herself, giver of wealth and prosperity.

"Where is she studying? She's three years old, isn't she?"

He nodded again, and mentioned the name of the little one-room school that his daughter attended. He expected May-dum to nod and send him on his way, but she didn't. Instead, she proceeded to ask him a great many questions about his life, and especially about his daughter.

Before he knew it, he was telling her everything. All his hopes, his dreams, his fondest wishes for his beloved Hema, and the despair that had dogged his footsteps these past few months. For how was he to continue to educate her with so many mouths to feed? His higher salary seemed to be eaten up just as quickly as his old one, in medical bills, and food, and most recently, the need to collect an amount large enough to marry off his younger sister. How could he possibly take care of Hema in the manner of his dreams?

Later, he'd emerged from May-dum's study in a curious state of horrified delirium. Horrified that he had divulged everything so freely, he who always kept his own counsel. Delirious, because May-dum had said that she would take care of little Hema's education herself. He was not to worry.

Furthermore, she said, she would like to see where the little girl studied, and could he please arrange a visit?

*   *   *

When his excitement had settled down, it had taken a full month for him and his family to organize things. His father had assumed generalship of the affair, and Raju let him. He himself was at work the whole day, and this was not a matter he could leave to his wife; she lacked the experience. She was not a man of the world.

Raju and his father would stay up late every evening, immersed in progress reviews: What should they do to the house? Could they afford to repaint it? Didn't so-and-so's brother-in-law work in a paint shop? Perhaps he could get some cheap color for them at a discount. And what would they offer her to eat? Would she consent to eat anything at all? Would she show them that respect? And how should they all dress? As if for a wedding? Or more casually? "Respectably," said Raju, to whom that word evoked the best images. "Respectably."

And so they had planned and arranged and organized. Raju spoke to his daughter's schoolteacher, who was awed and delighted at the prospect of a visit to her little school from such an important patron.

The day before the visit, he reviewed everything. And now, as he stood outside his employer's house, cleaning her car as never before, he acknowledged that the only unforeseeable, unplannable catch in the whole event was May-dum herself.

His family probably envisioned her as a routine memsahib, traditionally and expensively dressed, preaching morality and good family values. And—uniquely—acting upon them too. What if, after all his talk and boasting, she disgraced him? As only she could—carelessly, in the things that were to her utterly trivial, matters of dress and feminine comportment. He would still be loyal to her, but his pride and prestige in his family and neighborhood would be lost forever.

The car was cleaned and ready and polished. Instead of following his usual practice of going around to the kitchen for a cup of coffee, he stood waiting expectantly, staring at the door. Yesterday she had said that she would be ready to leave around ten o'clock. He still had almost forty-five minutes to go, but he didn't feel like wandering away, as if that might cause her to change her mind, or tempt her to sneak out of the house on foot or on her daughter's small bicycle.

At ten minutes past ten, his heart sank. He scolded himself for getting his hopes up, for expecting this visit to actually happen. He hadn't yet seen May-dum, but he'd seen enough to know that she wouldn't be going anywhere that morning. Just five minutes earlier, the bungalow gates had opened to allow a car to come through. It was May-dum's mother-in-law, come to pay a surprise visit. These could last anywhere from five minutes to a full day, depending on her mood and her daughter-in-law's quiescence.

The elder Mrs. Choudhary vanished in a blaze of satisfaction down the drive, exactly one hour later. Raju began to feel nervous all over again. Would May-dum decide to leave now, or would she decide it was too late and that they would have to postpone the whole thing till the next day? Would he be able to? His family had used precious water to scrub themselves clean that morning, and they were all instructed to be on their best behavior. His wife had prepared a sweet and a savory with ghee, the clarified butter that he had bought specially for the occasion. The food wouldn't last long in the hot weather. He didn't know if he could marshal all these resources for two days running.

Shanti the ayah appeared. "She wants you to bring the car to the porch," she said routinely. His heart skipped. He watched her walk back to the house, and was almost tempted to call her back. He hadn't yet confided in any of his colleagues about May-dum's proposed visit to his house. The very idea of it would be as startling to them as it was to him. Would they approve, or would they be envious? They were all good people, but Raju didn't want even a hint of a jealous, evil eye cast upon this visit. Let it happen, he told himself. Then he would tell everybody.

He drove the car around to the porch, watching the door and wondering once again how she would be dressed.

The door opened. He heard her voice call out to the cook to bring her a glass of cold water. Two minutes later she emerged. Raju almost laughed in delight and relief. She was wearing a lovely *salwar khameez,* the full-sleeved tunic flowing elegantly down to her calves, her ankles modestly covered by the loose pants below, the crisp, transparent, shawl-like *dupatta* draped and pleated over one shoulder. She looked like a movie star. Better than that, even, she looked every inch the memsahib.

She paused near the top of the steps and smiled in his direction. "Ready to go, Raju?"

Raju spent an hour and a half on two buses to get to and from work every day. The gleaming air-conditioned car did the same job in thirty minutes. The route took them away from the posh residential areas of the city, into and past industrial areas, and into regions that weren't really scaled for human consumption but had nevertheless been colonized by the hordes of workers who fed the appetites of a hungry city. As they neared his neighborhood, Raju kept glancing nervously into the rearview mirror. She was gazing intently out the window. What was she thinking? As he'd done for a month now, he tried to see his surroundings through her eyes.

"How much further to the school, Raju?"

"Hardly five minutes, May-dum."

She started asking him questions about the neighborhood, and as he had once before, Raju found himself talking freely to her. Housing ranged from slums to small single-room dwellings. There were few power connections, even fewer legal ones. The water supply was haphazard. The buses, thankfully, ran fairly close to the area—he could catch one into the city just a half kilometer away from his house.

He turned off the main road and immediately encountered a problem—one that he hadn't foreseen. The road changed from asphalt to muddy pathways ravaged by the rains. The people who lived here usually either walked or traveled on twowheelers that could slither and slide and navigate their way through these roads that were never intended for heavy fourwheel traffic. Raju inched the car along, feeling it slip down muddy slopes and miniature sand crevasses, hearing the wheels catch and spin in the mud. He had a horrible vision of getting his employer and her car stuck here, and forcing her to walk in the hot, muddy road. He shifted into the lowest gears and concentrated on getting the car down the side of the sloping hill. At the bottom lay the school. A little further on, his home.

They were two hours later than planned. Raju parked the car and escorted May-dum to the door, where the schoolteacher immediately appeared, ready and waiting for them. Raju noticed that the room inside was a little cleaner than usual. The chairs were in a straight line. The twelve little children who studied with his daughter were dressed smartly, in clothes that were cleaner than their stained faces and dusty hair; a few were in newly acquired blue-and-white uniforms. There was a new map on the wall. A chair had been placed next to the teacher's, so May-dum would have somewhere to sit. He glanced briefly at his own daughter. She was staring openmouthed at May-dum, as were all the children. He was pleased to see that she was the best-dressed child in the class, but that was natural. For months now, she'd worn nothing but May-dum's daughter's castaways: best-quality outfits, thick sweaters, sturdy shoes—clothes that made Raju's heart squeeze with pleasure when he saw his daughter in them.

He went out to wait by the car. He could hear the murmur of voices as May-dum talked with the teacher, and then the shrill sounds of the children as they were put through their paces in front of their audience: spelling, geography. In Kannada and in English. And finally, their mathematical tables, recited in a mono-tone: vun-toojh-a-too, vun-theejh-a-thee, vun-fojh-a-fo.

May-dum followed him out fifteen minutes later, her face pensive. Her voice, though, was brisk. "I have paid your daughter's school fees for the entire year. In return, the teacher should provide her with books, two sets of uniforms, pencils. Please see that she does do all of that. Let me know if she doesn't."

"She will," said Raju. "She is a good woman. A good teacher." After a pause, he said awkwardly, "May-dum, thank you so much for this. It is a great kindness on your part."

"It's nothing," she said. "I am happy to do it. Now, Raju, do I get to meet your wife?"

He grinned and held the door open. "Yes, May-dum."

The visit was as he had hoped it would be. She didn't let him down.

From the time the car stopped outside his house, he knew. It was written in the manner of her walk, her look of interest, her polite and gentle words to his father, who was waiting at the door. It was in some oblique way a reciprocation—for all the times he had anticipated her movements and moved in concert with her expectations. Now it seemed she was doing the same for him.

He watched his father usher her into their house. She paused at the door and, respectfully, slipped off her shoes.

"May-dum, you don't have to do that!"

"That's all right," she said.

Raju was later glad that his father seamlessly took charge. He watched May-dum being escorted to the bench inside, where she sat down. He watched her join her palms in greeting to his mother and his wife, and then make animated, interested conversation with his parents as though they were acquaintances that she might meet at the Club. He felt his cheeks burn as May-dum praised him to his family. His wife vanished into the kitchen, presumably to reemerge with refreshments, but she never did. Raju went in after her and found her waiting there nervously, a hot tumbler of coffee prepared and a plate with the sweet and the savory ready to serve.

"Go on," he muttered to her.

"No. You do it," she whispered back, shaking her head.

"Don't be silly," he said, but he saw that she really was too shy. So, in a facsimile of the tray that Julie the cook used, he picked up a metal plate, placed the food and coffee on it, and took it out.

"Oh! So much trouble!" his May-dum said. "Really, you shouldn't have."

"No, no. Please eat," they murmured.

Raju's mother, with a feeling of duty done, joined her daughter-in-law in the kitchen with great relief. Raju could see them peeping at May-dum from behind the curtain that hung in front of the door. So it was Raju's father who chatted with May-dum: Yes, it was a nice little house, two rooms and a kitchen for the six of them, but the rents were too high and increasing every year. Their landlord lived next door, and had built two more houses just like this down the road. He was a lucky man, great foresight, to have bought this land when it was cheap. Perhaps someday Raju would be able to do so also. Already, in this one year of his employment, they had been able to acquire a radio and a black-and-white TV. They were grateful, deeply grateful. He didn't mention that the house had been painted this clean, bright pink just a week ago, or that this impromptu living room was usually cluttered with the mess of living, now shoved into the room next door. Now, in addition to two benches, it had the pink walls, clean curtains, the pooja altar, and the TV.

Raju watched May-dum eat. She finished all her coffee, and ate enough of the sweet and the savory to indicate that they were nice, to her taste, not beneath her at all. She praised the food, and Raju could hear his wife giggling with pleasure inside the kitchen.

When they finally stepped outside, Raju could see that word had spread. The road was filled with neighbors, all watching him, May-dum, and the car with unabashed curiosity. May-dum slipped on her shoes and said her good-byes to his family, and then paused outside the car instead of climbing in immediately. With every eye upon them, she exchanged a few pleasant words with him with a casual air that provoked his neighbors to ask him, even a week after the visit: "So, what did she say to you then?" to which Raju would shrug and say, "Nothing special." And that would impress them even more.

On the drive back into the city, they continued to chat about his family. May-dum praised his home and his parents, and Raju filled her in on his sister, and their plans for her marriage. He found himself talking easily, and was surprised that he hadn't really ventured to earlier.

"If you need any assistance with your sister's wedding, please speak to me about it."

"I will, May-dum."

"And please do see to it that your daughter's schoolteacher provides all the things that she has promised. . . ."

Raju nodded. He would do that. Raju turned the car into the Club. He wanted to thank May-dum again for all her kindness, and also for the courtesy of her visit, but her attention was suddenly distracted.

"Tara! . . . Raju, stop the car."

May-dum's friend looked at her elegant dress in surprise as she got out of the car.

"Oh, my! Look at you! Where have you been?"

"Visiting," said May-dum.

He watched her for a minute, walking away towards the main clubhouse, one arm linked loosely around her friend's and listening appreciatively to some anecdote; then Raju-once-Rangappa climbed back into his seat behind the wheel, shifted into first gear, and swung the car slowly around the flowered lawns and up to the parking lot, where all the drivers waited until they were summoned.

ALPHABET
SOUP

Priyamvada knew that her father was, once again, not listening to her.

She was used to it, however, this paternal preoccupation with things that didn't matter, so she didn't let it put her off her stride. She was speaking on her favorite topic: what sounded (to the inattentive ear) like a discourse on art and the impact of yellows, browns, and blacks on red, white, and blue, but was, in fact, all about race relations and American politics.

Her parents had just finished dinner, and were relaxing in the family living room in Chicago, surrounded by the artifacts of a well-sprung suburban life. Her mother was absorbed, insensate, in *People* magazine; Priya flipped through an old favorite, the *Guinness World Records*, 1984 edition, and tried to grab her father's attention as it wandered between the golf being played on the television screen and her mother's occasional interjections on family and neighborhood gossip.

★ ★ ★

Priya's father had moved his fledgling family from India to America when she was a baby, and for the first eighteen years of her life Priya had somehow blamed herself for being brown in a country where the popular icons were all Pale-Shades-of-Pink.

Her very first year at an elite East Coast school (tuition bills sent to her father, pizza bills sent to her), Priya munched on strawberries, sipped champagne, pondered the academic life choices open to her (archeologist? accountant? anthropologist? shaman? earth mother? computer-age hero?), signed petitions complaining about the college cafeteria ("the sushi sucks!"), and—finally—learned the vocabulary of political victimhood.

Now, when asked, Priya still referred to herself as a student. Of life, she usually added, but only in her mind. Reluctant to graduate, the fact was she enjoyed nesting in the cerebral comforts of an American university, moving eagerly from her undergraduate studies to a master's program, and now toying with the idea of working towards a doctorate in something else altogether. Through it all, she had never allowed herself to forget that:

a) as a Person of Color in America, she was hopelessly Disenfranchised, and

b) that it was up to the System to do something about it.

She could but complain.

That is, until she one day was confronted by the true epiphany of every student of political activism, printed on a piece of paper and stuck, right there, on her professor's door: THINK GLOBAL, the sign said. ACT LOCAL.

Local, for Priya, was her parents, and for several years she acted upon them, trying to drag them up to her level, but with very limited success. "Assimilation is a betrayal of your skin," Priya explained to her father more than once.

"How can it be a betrayal of your skin to work hard and do well?"

"Do well—at what *cost*? And on whose *terms*?"

Her father looked around their home (five bedrooms, swimming pool, three-car garage) and smiled. "It's nice that you have the luxury of your opinions," he said.

Which was no answer at all.

Her mother remained equally impervious to her multicultural obligations. She loyally supported her husband in his Americanized life (even without the testosterone to excuse her bad judgment): cutting her hair short, dressing in suits and skirts, abstaining from any prayers or special Indian rituals, and working hard to eliminate all traces of melody from her accent. She had almost succeeded, but she would never sound like her daughter, who, like her, had the facial features of a tropical rice-eater, but who opened her mouth and was pure corn-fed Chicago. (Alas, her mother's reluctance to embrace a higher quality of life extended to other areas as well: she wouldn't abandon her vegetarianism to join in Priya's recent experiment with veganism, and, for that matter, refused to run with wolves, free her inner child, live in integrity with her spirit, or even indulge in some straightforward vaginal mirror-gazing, meeting all such requests with a simple: "What nonsense!")

Undaunted, Priya focused her efforts on her father. Not for nothing was she a member of the Color Coalition and the Wymyns' Alliance. "The mistake you made," she told him, "was in moving to America all those years ago."

"You would have preferred to grow up in India?" Priya's father was tall and thin, with a receding hairline and eyes hidden behind thick glasses, which sometimes made his daughter miss the twinkle that lay deep in them.

"The more I think about it . . . yes," said Priyamvada. "There is a strength in being Brown in a Brown Country."

"And what is that?"

"Well, look at the way we're treated here."

"Meritocratic promotions, good education, nice homes?" He didn't say it, but Priya knew he also meant: his country club membership, his partnership in a multinational accounting firm, and the fact that both his children studied in universities that had groomed American presidents.

"Not that stuff," she said. "You're always focusing on material comforts, ignoring everything else. Here in America, nice stores treat whites better, and blondes best. In a brown country, everyone looks at each other with respect and feels the bond that comes from having the same color skin. There, there is a sense of pride about their own history, a refusal to cater to eurocentric notions of the world, a joy that comes from being perfectly centered culturally . . . Are you *laughing*?"

"No, no," her father said, hastily.

"You are. I can't believe this. You're not taking me seriously. . . . Is he, Ma? . . . He's belittling me. Isn't he? Ma?"

"Yes, yes," said her mother absently. "I mean, no, sweetie. Of course not . . . Do you want to watch that new movie with me? Julia Roberts and that other fellow, I-forget-his-name. You know," her mother said, returning to her magazine, "if you comb your hair the way she does, you'd look very pretty."

Priyamvada slammed the *Guinness World Records* shut. "I can't believe this."

"Come on, Priya," her father said. "You've got to understand, there is a vast gap between the social theories they preach in the universities and the realities outside. You've got to understand this. . . . Maybe if you put your intelligence and education to work in a practical sphere you'd understand what I mean."

"You're saying I don't know what I'm talking about," said Priya. "What am I, stupid?"

"No, no," said her father. "Not stupid at all."

"And what's so damn impractical about what I'm doing now? What am I, a space cadet?"

Priyamvada saw her father hesitate, and she coldly decided not to pursue the conversation any further. But her father still had the parting word: "If you're so sure of your ideas," he said, "why don't you go visit India and see for yourself?"

Priya was startled. Her last visit to India had been when she was a sulky five-year-old; she and her brother had subsequently never joined her mother on those annual pilgrimages she made to a place, twenty years on, still referred to as Home. (Priya was used to her mother's careful sophistry: "Let's go home" meant their house in Chicago; "I'm going Home," with that extra little resonance, meant a visit to South India, to Bangalore, where she'd grown up.)

The idea festered in her brain as she returned to college, and to the arms of her boyfriend. Eric was, regrettably, not dark-skinned, but he was very colorful, with naturally orange hair, blue eyes, and brown freckles atop pink skin that flushed a deep red in moments of intellectual excitement; indeed, a veritable Coalition of Colors, all in himself, along with the sort of muscles that looked, Priya thought fondly, as though he spent his days working with his hands, close to the earth. "I do wish, though," Priya had once wistfully told her mother during a dinner at home, "that I were a lesbian." To be Officially Oppressed by gender, skin color, *and* sexuality would be no ordinary distinction.

Tchi, her mother had said. What a horrible thing to say.

"Perhaps," her father had said, "you could dress your young man in a frock. In drag, as you say. Then you could at least be a lesbian couple."

Both Priya and her mother had turned reproachful gazes at him, though for different reasons.

But despite his inherent limitations, Eric was a credit to her. When not bench-pressing at the gym, or working with other friends at the Tree Hugger's Café (where Everything was Recycled, including, Priya suspected, the food), he spent his time protesting innovatively, usually against the World Trade Organization. He was rather an expert in the art of collecting signatures.

"I think it's a great idea," he said enthusiastically, when she'd finished exploring the contents of his underwear to her satisfaction. "We can ride the trains, third-class, around the smaller cities of India, then perhaps work in a forest conservation program for a few weeks, and end our visit with a week of meditation in an ashram."

Priya paused. Her notion of standing, shortly, in a world where the color of the skin on the street matched hers, did not, for some reason, include having a pink-and-orange man by her side (however well muscled).

"You know, you really shouldn't bother coming with me,"

she said. "You should go do that Greenpeace thing, like you'd planned. They need you there."

Yes, he said, flexing his muscles meditatively. I think you're right. But you should follow the program I suggested, he said. Don't do just the tourist stuff.

Priya threw herself into planning the trip with her customary fervor and attention to detail. She read guidebooks, she surfed the Web. As an afterthought, she spoke to her parents.

"Do the Delhi–Agra–Jaipur triangle," said her father, as he did to anyone who planned to see India. "Some really lovely things there. The Taj Mahal. Palaces. Maybe you'll even get to see a snake charmer or some dancing bears. Nice hotels," he added, "so you don't have to deal with the dust and the dirt."

Priya shrugged her shoulders in unfilial irritation. That was her father all over. Completely missing the point.

"I don't want to see the tourist stuff. I want to experience the real India. . . . You know, it would be so great if I could actually stay in someone's home instead of in a hotel."

"That's easily arranged," her mother said. "If that's what you want."

And so her itinerary fell into place. Priya didn't have any immediate aunts or uncles in India; all of her parents' siblings were scattered across the globe, in America, Canada, England, and Australia, returning to India only for annual pilgrimages along with her mother. Priya would be staying, therefore, with distant relatives in Bangalore: Mr. and Mrs. Iyer; her mother's cousin's husband's sister, strangely enough, married to her father's second cousin.

"That's not a relation at all," she told her mother.

"No, no," her mother said. "We're very close. The Iyers will look after you well. Such fun it will be!" her mother said. "I wish I were coming with you."

Her father simply said: If things in India are not as you imagine, promise me that, when you return, we will have a serious chat about your future.

Oh, don't worry, said Priya, shrugging off the seriousness in his voice. They will be.

Priyamvada packed her bags carefully, mindful of the advice she'd read in the *Lonely Planet* guidebook ("Modesty rates highly in India"). She took long pants, full-sleeved shirts, and skirts that fell below her knees. She even went one step further and raided her mother's closet, the very thought of which would once have shocked her. (Among other things, Priya and her mother disagreed on dress.) But to her mother's closet she went and unearthed the special section her mother reserved for her own trips to India: full of sarees and salwar-khameez suits.

"I don't think I'll take any sarees," she told her mother.

"No, you most certainly will not," said her mother, staring indignantly at the pile of salwar-khameez outfits that Priya had selected.

She flew to New York and spent a celebratory night with friends. She barely made the airport the next morning, avoiding (by inches) complete annihilation by a passing yellow cab, whose driver cursed her in a colorful New York–Jamaican patois.

"Yeah, *yours,* motherfucker," Priya yelled back, in a show of unity with the colored peoples of the world, and waved good-bye to America.

"It is a truth, universally acknowledged," said Mr. Iyer, "that brahmins are clean, disciplined, and intellectual. You are agreeing with me?"

A voice in Priyamvada's mind begged to differ, but she stifled it. Mr. Iyer, she already knew, didn't really expect a response from her. He liked to ask a profound question ("What means brahminism?") and immediately answer it himself ("You see, there is a cultural aspect, and a philosophical aspect . . ."), sweeping aside any interim waste-of-time discussion period. Conversation, for Mr. Iyer, was a one-man dialectic played to an attentive audience.

She had wondered, at first, if he was bothered by her incessant questions, but he had quickly reassured her. He enjoyed sharing his knowledge, he said, with a Bright Young Person. It reminded him of his days as an Indian Railways bureaucrat.

"Clean," she said now. "You mean, like, baths and stuff?"

"Oh, no. Well, that is to say, baths, definitely. But much more . . . It is a glorious tradition," Mr. Iyer said. "It is, after all, brahmins who have given the world the concept of zero, and yoga, and the philosophies that underlie Vedantic and Buddhist thinking. And it is all linked—the notions of cleanliness, personal discipline, and intellectual thinking. Holistic," he said, relishing the word. "Is it not?"

As before, Priya nodded reluctantly. There was some rule, she knew, about observing native behavior without interfering. Was that out of her sociology classes or from *Star Trek*? She couldn't remember, but she decided to play it safe and say nothing. She quieted her unease by reminding herself that Mr. Iyer was talking of times gone by. The caste system, relic of India's cultural past, had nothing to do with the whole modern Mahatma Gandhi *liberté, égalité, fraternité* thing, pardon her French.

"And next week," said Mr. Iyer, "you will be seeing a function that celebrates that very essence."

In a movie? asked Priya.

"In my cousin's house," said Mr. Iyer. "It is time for his son's *poonal* ceremony. The thread ceremony. It is only a ritual, of course, nothing more, but you are most welcome to attend. After all, you are not seeing such things in America. Also, the ceremony is an invocation to knowledge, and with your academic background, you will enjoy."

Mr. Iyer, Priya knew, utterly approved of her dedication to the academic life. It was one of the things she liked about him. "Ah yes, a PhD," he had said, pleased. "Your mother said. It is a good thing." In his view, a bachelor's degree alone was no education at all, and fit only for foreigners, perverts, and other deviants. He liked to moralize about a young woman of his acquaintance (his cousin's neighbor's daughter) who, perhaps due to some environmental oversight, had suddenly decided to abandon the banking job and the MBA course applications that had so gladdened her parents' hearts, and to write books instead. "Storybooks," said Mr. Iyer. "And they say she has also started smoking."

His own children were excessively educated: his son a lawyer and living in Delhi, his daughter with a PhD in computer science and now working in a software company in the fabled Electronic City that had attached itself like a pimple to Bangalore's bum.

"She is in BPO," said Mr. Iyer, with his usual love of acronyms. "She and her husband also. BPO for banks."

"Business process outsourcing," Mrs. Iyer later explained, with the air of someone who has carefully committed the phrase to memory.

Mr. Iyer lived a quiet life with his wife in the Bangalore suburb of Malleswaram. Their house was small, single-storied, and flat-roofed; painted a dust-covered white, separated from the road by bits of broken pavement and an open ditch, and from the neighboring houses by six inches of air and a compound wall. Haphazard black wires snaked dangerously over and into the house, and provided cable television.

Inside, the house was very clean, and rather spartan. A living room, a dining room, bedrooms with attached bathrooms that contained no shower or tub, but instead a bucket placed below hot- and cold-water taps, and a mug to sluice oneself with. In Priya's bathroom, as a concession, Mrs. Iyer had placed a roll of toilet paper on the shelf, alongside a bar of Rexona soap still in its lime-green paper wrapping, a tube of Colgate toothpaste, and an orange-and-white tin of Cuticura talcum powder.

The furnishings were plain, a triumph of function over form. Cane furniture on the verandah, Rexene-covered sofas surrounding the small synthetic carpet in the living room, a melamine-laminated table in the dining room. There was a cheerful carelessness in the placement of a calendar here and a photograph there. Art was represented in solitary splendor by a Tanjore painting of the god Krishna as an infant, wearing nothing but a smile, some jewelry, and a peacock feather in his hair, the divine testicles picked out in pink and gold. Blue plastic flowers in a vase; a television; two wooden bookshelves, one filled with encyclopedias and books from *Reader's Digest,* the other stacked with the Tamil magazines that Mrs. Iyer enjoyed, invariably depicting pink-cheeked, long-haired females wearing sarees that threatened to slip off the slopes of their plump bosoms. On a corner table, competing with the television for pride of place, was the computer, a fancy model bought for them by their children; maintained with pristine reverence, used for e-mails and correspondence, and kept carefully enclosed, when not in use, in thick white plastic covers.

Mr. and Mrs. Iyer, Priya soon discovered, kept time to a different rhythm from the rest of the world. They awoke early and cheerfully in a hungover world; they prayed with unfashionable devotion; their vegetarianism was ancient, not trendy. Yet they were not precisely immune to outside influences: Mr. Iyer spent his days snorting over the contents of the newspapers, while Mrs. Iyer never missed her evening television, one hour of a Tamil soap opera that dealt, it seemed, with Family Anguish— cruel mothers-in-law, rebellious daughters, sons who wouldn't show respect, in a world where Fate, it seemed, continually thwarted Desire. Mrs. Iyer would click her tongue in sympathy, while Mr. Iyer snorted in derision. Priya's eyes would swivel between the television and the soft syncopating mutter of clicks and snorts.

Priya could not help being fascinated. The Iyers still adhered faithfully to the conservative Tamil Brahmin lifestyle that her parents had forsaken to immerse themselves in Money and Mc-Nuggets. This was how things Might Have Been in her own family. Mr. Iyer was her own father's Alternate Reality. The two men were even similar in face and build, except that Mr. Iyer lacked the spit-and-polish conveyed by Americanization, Italian suits, and hundred-dollar haircuts.

Mr. Iyer liked to sit on the verandah, on a swing made from a sturdy plank of rosewood, leaving his wife to bustle about the house and occasionally step out with tumblers of piping hot coffee. He himself was retired and spent his days reading his newspapers in a skirt.

"Not a skirt," he said, pained when Priya first phrased her careful inquiry. "Not a skirt at all. It is a *veshti*. A *lungi*, a *dhoti*. Men's wear. Just like suitings, shirtings, and cuff links. But," he said, "more comfortable for the heat."

"Oh, a sarong," said Priya.

"No," said Mr. Iyer. "A veshti."

As with all of Mr. Iyer's utterances, Priya made a note of this in her diary that evening. "A veshti," she wrote, "is a long piece of cotton cloth worn wrapped around the waist. Sometimes it can be folded in half at the knee. It is similar" a postscript added in defiance of Mr. Iyer, "to the Southeast Asian sarong."

That evening she sent an e-mail to her father.

She wrote: "Have you ever worn a veshti? They seem very comfortable. Would you like me to bring one back for you?"

He wrote back: Yes I have. They are indeed. Do bring one back. I'm sure it will be a big hit with the other partners in the Chicago office.

*   *   *

Now, Mrs. Iyer joined them on the verandah where they sat, shaded from the Saturday morning sun. "Anasuya called," she said. "She is on her way over. Are you ready?"

Priya nodded. Anasuya was Mrs. Iyer's niece (about Priya's age, Mrs. Iyer had said), and about to take Priya for an outing. "You will enjoy so much." Mrs. Iyer said, "Meeting some youngsters. You cannot only be sitting with us old people. So boring for you."

Priya was carefully and conservatively dressed for this excursion, in a long-sleeved shirt and a skirt that ended around her ankles. She knew better than to inflict her American ways upon these people. She would act with decorum and sobriety. Though, already, a week of abstinence from smoking was giving her a headache and a marked impulse to bite passing strangers in the ankles.

A small tallboy car came to a halt in front of the house. A young woman got out, and, watching her, Priya was immediately glad of the way she had dressed. Anasuya was wearing jeans, which were covered to the knee by a long kurta shirt, full sleeved and high collared. Her long hair was tied back in a ponytail. She waved cheerfully towards the verandah.

"Do you want coffee?" her aunt asked her as she approached. "This is Priyamvada."

"Hi," said Anasuya. "Nice to meet you. And no, thanks, Sundari Chithi. I got hungry, so I bought something to eat." She came to a halt in front of the verandah and waved a plastic bag at her aunt.

"Come in," said Mr. Iyer. "Anu is in public relations," he told Priya. "Doing very well, very well. Come in."

Anu shook her head. "After I finish this," she said, sitting down on the front steps.

Mrs. Iyer peered suspiciously at the green bag, from which Anu pulled out a chapati roll filled with something spicy. "You bought something? But I could have made something for you quickly. . . . You should not eat that rubbish. Chicken, onions, garlic—I can smell the stink of it all the way here."

"It's delicious," Anu said, with a grin. "Want a bite?"

"Tchi, tchi! You please wash your hands afterwards." Mrs. Iyer bustled away to make coffee.

"Your aunt is right," said Mr. Iyer. "You should not eat these foods. Vegetarianism is not only part of your brahmin heritage, it is also very fashionable today, is it not? Priyamvada here is vegetarian."

Vegan, Priya wanted to say, but she had brought it up once before, and Mrs. Iyer had looked at her mystified and said, Wagon? and Priya had not felt up to explaining.

"You've convinced my mind, Vasu Chittappa," said Anu. "Now you just have to convince my tongue." She bit into her chapati roll.

"Work is going well? Is that a new car?" asked Mr. Iyer, looking at the tallboy parked in front of the gate.

"Yes," said Anu. "But I bought it secondhand, for a good price. Very cheap. Very low mileage, too, so it worked out well."

"How so? If it has low mileage, why are they not asking a good price for it? Perhaps they have tricked you. All sorts of cheap *goondas* are doing anything to make money these days."

"No, no," said Anu. "You know these people. Mrs. Ranganathan?"

Mrs. Iyer emerged, carrying a tray of coffee steaming gently in steel tumblers, and caught the last bit of the conversation.

"That woman! Mrs. Ranganathan," she said. "Thinking she is the only one with good news in this world. As though our children are not doing well. Here, drink it while it is hot." Mrs. Iyer sat down next to her husband on the long wooden swing and used one of his newspapers to fan herself. "And she cannot talk about anything else. Even when I went to give her sweets after our son got that job. No time for my happiness, only, oh, see how well Sita does. . . . But what else to expect? That woman is an Iyengar, after all."

"Iyengar?" Priya asked as she drank her coffee. Hot and milky and sweet, it was very different from the black coffee she preferred.

"Tamil Brahmins," said Mr. Iyer. "Just like us Iyers. Same caste, but a subsect, so to speak."

"Nonsense! Not just like us! We Iyers are different. Those Iyengars do things all wrong," Mrs. Iyer explained. "Like sometimes putting coconut in their *rasam*."

Mr. Iyer snorted. Mrs. Iyer ignored him and leaned forward. "Frankly," she said, "they are not supposed to be as intelligent as us."

"Oh, yes," her husband concurred happily. "We're supposed to be the brainy ones, while they have all the good looks."

Mrs. Iyer smoothed her hair back defiantly. "Well, I don't know about *that*," she said, "but we are definitely brighter. Why are you talking about Mrs. Ranganathan, anyway?"

"I bought Sita's car," said Anu. "She gave me a great deal on it. I think she's buying a new one, something larger."

"What is that?" said Mrs. Iyer, shocked. "You bought her car secondhand? But this is not right! What are we, poor people to take their castoffs?"

"Well, I think it's okay," said Anu. "I mean, it's not as if she's gifting it to me; I paid good money for it."

"Tchi, tchi. This is not a right thing to do. I am going to speak to your mother about this. And does she know about this chicken-eating?"

Priya responded immediately to the mute appeal in Anu's eyes. "I'm ready when you are," she said. Anu stood hastily. Priya held her hand out. "I can take that for you, if you like," she said, reaching out for the plastic bag that contained the debris of Anu's snack. "I'll throw it away in the kitchen."

"Oh no!" three people chorused, and Priya froze, her hand still extended.

Anu laughed. "Sorry about that, but my aunt is quite strict in her *madi* practices, you know."

"No, no. Not strict at all. How things used to be in the old days! Now we are all quite relaxed."

Anu caught the look of confusion in Priya's face and explained. "You know, stuff like not even carrying a wee bit of non-veg food into the house. No onions, no garlic. No alcohol or cigarettes . . . that sort of thing. I'll have to throw away this bag in the rubbish dump at the end of the street."

"Oh, right," said Priya. "I knew that."

"But we are not strict at all," said Mrs. Iyer, appealing to her husband. "We are quite modern."

"Well, certainly, in traditional terms, we are not following all the madi rules," Mr. Iyer said. "When I was a boy, things were quite different."

"Vasu Chittappa, things couldn't possibly have been stricter than in this house," Anu teased. "Shall we go? Would you like me to fetch anything for you from the shops, Chithi?"

"No, no, thank you, *kanna*. You go now. Enjoy yourselves," said Mrs. Iyer. "And when you come back, I shall keep some ice cream in the fridge for you."

"And that," said Anasuya, putting her arm around Mrs. Iyer, "is my dear aunt being gay to dissipation."

They climbed into the car and drove away. When they turned the street corner, Anasuya parked the car next to an overflowing rubbish bin and threw the plastic bag away. When she was done, she didn't set the car in motion immediately. As Priya watched, she shrugged out of her kurta shirt, revealing a tank top tucked into her jeans below. Then she removed the rubber band that tied her hair together and shook her head until the hair flowed free over her shoulders. She opened her handbag and pulled on a pair of shades.

"Ah," she said, looking at herself in the little rearview mirror. "That's better."

Mrs. Iyer threw her hostessing energies into organizing sightseeing and shopping expeditions for Priya; Mr. Iyer, from his post on the verandah, simply offered his services as an encyclopedic reference point on any subject that Priya cared to name. Brahminism and the caste system; the willfully malingering government; the misuse of monosodium glutamate in Chinese cooking; the operational differences between jungle bandits in South India and the ravine *dacoits* of Madhya Pradesh; yoga; genome theory and the implications of Dolly the cloned sheep on the Australian economy (footnotes on New Zealand included); and why America's corporate scandals were caused, in part, by a lack of meditative self-awareness in its chief executive officers, and further exacerbated by improper breathing techniques.

At some point in her college career, Priya had done some reading about India's caste history, and decided that she would really have preferred to be a "Dalit," a member of the lowest castes, who, in the past fifty years, had gone through a major regenerative process of empowerment, finding their political voice, their cultural voice, and deep inner strength. It was the kind of story that inspired her, and made her want to claim it as her own. Instead she was stuck with an ancestry of oppression.

She asked Mr. Iyer: "So brahmins were at the top of the caste rankings, right? Even above kings?"

"Yes," said Mr. Iyer. "No other culture in the world has placed respect for intellectual and spiritual prowess over military and money. Is it not wonderful? It is a glorious tradition."

Priya remembered the conversation with Anu. "What, exactly, are madi rules?"

"Madi. Ah, yes. You see," said Mr. Iyer, "traditionally, the brahmin lifestyle was very simple and austere. Brahmins felt that spiritual and intellectual growth could not be achieved without personal discipline and austerity. . . . Stress was laid on ahimsa, or nonviolence, sensual control, cleanliness. So, of course, no meat, and no foods that stimulate the senses, such as garlic, onion, and heavy spices. Time was spent in academic and intellectual pursuits and daily study of the Vedanta scriptures and sutras. And also in the practice of yoga, and meditation. Within the house, this led to the rigorous cleanliness practices known as madi. One could not do anything, no cooking, no morning worship, no eating, without first bathing. And after that, to promote hygiene, one could not have any physical contact with germ-ridden unbathed persons, or an unwashed cloth. That was why, in daytime, we rested on wooden pillows. In the kitchen, food had to be prepared fresh for each meal, and only in near-sterilized cooking conditions. Very strict kitchen . . ." he searched his mind ". . . protocol. Extremely scientific, is it not?"

"Right," said Priya. Why had *Lonely Planet* made no mention of this? "So none of these practices are followed today?"

"No, no. Only a few. And in Anasuya's generation, sorry to say, even less. Clean practices they are, holistic, and very important to a spiritual life, but impractical to maintain nowadays, one travels so much, eats out in restaurants and what-not. Of course, when my mother was alive, we could not deviate at all. She was very strict. Just as your grandmother used to be."

Priya had seen photographs of her grandmother, a plump, smiling woman with her well-oiled hair smoothed into a bun and dressed with jasmine flowers. For the first time, Priya wondered how this woman had accepted her children's transition from an environment like this to a turkey-basting, pig-part-eating, cow-rump-grilling country that equated success with material and sensual excess.

"So the brahmins, like, had all the other castes waiting on them hand and foot?"

"No, no," said Mr. Iyer, genuinely shocked. "Of course not. What is this rubbish."

"They didn't?"

"Oh no," said Mr. Iyer. "In fact, to maintain their austere and disciplined lifestyle, it was considered important to limit contact with other castes and communities. At least, physical contact."

"Why?" said Priya. "Why was it so exclusionary?"

"You are curious about your cultural roots," Mr. Iyer beamed. "That is a good thing. Your mother has raised you well. Despite the fact," he said, "that many other castes also practiced high levels of cleanliness, it was considered best to keep contact with them to the minimal level, to prevent contamination and risk of bad social influences. Later, of course, this notion became ritualized, is it not, the scientific basis was forgotten, and only the stigma of pollution remained, and eventually, the social laws forbade any physical contact between brahmin and non-brahmin whatsoever."

But that's terrible, she said.

Mr. Iyer twinkled at her. "You are not the only one to think so," he said.

In the car, Anasuya had played Scott Joplin on the music system, telling Priya that the ragtime piano recording was by a friend. "You'll meet him now," she said. Priya had listened to the music, staring at the cotton skirt that covered her legs voluminously, clumsily. "I think you'll like them," said Anu, as though sensing her need for reassurance. "They're nice people."

Later, Priya had written a few e-mails.

To her friends at the Tree Hugger's Café, she wrote: I met some people our age in a social setting, and it was such a pleasure to see that they spanned the spectrum of India: punjabi, keralite, bengali, christian, muslim, brahmin, sitting together in a spirit of great communal accord and brotherhood.

She did not mention that this meeting had taken place in a coffeehouse that looked like an upmarket Starbucks, and that the women were dressed in tank tops and in skirts that ended mid-thigh; that the men had argued over the relative aesthetics of Jennifer Lopez and Britney Spears, and everybody seemed to be recovering from a hangover. That would be unnecessary local color and would simply muddy the issue.

She sent the same message to Eric, along with a paragraph on how much she missed him and his muscular body (A Lot).

To her father, she was even more circumspect. She wrote: The weather here is lovely. Cool, but with blue skies. I went out today with Mrs. Iyer's niece, Anasuya, and some of her friends. I met a young man who works in Bangalore, but in the same firm that you do.

"From that fact alone," her father wrote back, "I can tell he must be a very nice person."

He was. They had all been very pleasant and welcoming.

"Enjoying your holiday?" asked the young man, who'd been introduced to her as Farhan and also as the piano player.

"Oh yes," she said. "It's all very interesting."

He nodded. "Lots of ABCDs like you wandering around these days. It's the changing economic climate."

She'd heard that phrase before: ABCD—American Born Confused Desi. *Desi*, countryman. Her parents, despite having lived in America for over three decades, were FOB—Fresh off the Boat. There were jokes about ABCDs, which Priya did not find amusing: Have you heard of the ABCDEFGHI? American Born Confused Desi Emigrated From Gujarat Hall-the-vay-frum India.

"I may pretend to be an accountant," Farhan confided, when she asked. "But actually I'm a world-famous jazz musician, living incognito." He did an impromptu drumroll on the table with the coffee stirrers.

"You work in the same firm as my father," Priya told him, strangely unsettled.

"Oh yeah?" he said. "Well, me and half the world."

Now, two days later, Priyamvada nudged the floor with one foot to set the swing swaying gently on the Iyers' verandah. Just so must her grandmother have sat on a warm evening. Across the road, construction workers dug up a section of the pavement to lay broadband Internet cabling, their bare backs darkened by the sun and corded with ropy muscles, almost, it seemed, as if they spent their lives sunning on beaches and working out in health clubs.

Fatigue built within her. She longed, for an instant, to be back home, to be in environments familiar and well structured, where her accent would not make people gawk or say, excuse me? Where she was understood, and where she understood the world she lived in. She felt, right now, like learning nothing more than the ancient Indian art of Leisure; to sit down and let the world drift by, to let knowledge arrive when it was good and ready rather than rushing out in search of it. The whole enlightenment-buddha thing. Instead, Mr. Iyer wanted her to attend this poonal, this thread ceremony function.

Priya felt herself fidget. "Are you sure," she asked again, "that none of this caste system stuff is applicable today? Really?"

Mr. Iyer clicked his tongue, much as his wife did before the television. "Why do you concern yourself needlessly with all this? Once upon a time, it influenced our entire society, it is true. It divided, it excluded, is it not? But now, it has lost its sting. So in actual fact, it is now nothing more than a simple cultural practice, retained in a few homes." He quoted from his latest letter to the newspaper editor: " 'The need of the hour is more jobs, education, and drinking water.' Caste is a dead issue." He smiled reflectively. "In fact, some people argue that, nowadays, it is the brahmins who are being discriminated against, but that's another story."

"You should come," said Mrs. Iyer suddenly. She had joined them halfway through her dinner preparations. A large flat tray rested on her lap with uncooked rice mounded on one side. As she conversed, her eyes remained on the rice tray, inspecting it rigorously for stones and insects as her fingers lightly brushed the rice, a few grains at a time, from one side of the tray to the other. After cleaning the rice, she would wash it three times in water before steaming it in the pressure cooker. "You can meet many people, many relations and friends of your parents. And besides, of course, our niece Anasuya will be there too. You had a good time with her, no?"

"Yeah, I did. She'll be there?" Priyamvada said, startled.

In the café, Anu had offered Priya a cigarette. Priya's hand reached for it, but she stopped herself. Anu laughed. "Yeah, you better not. If she smells the smoke on you," she said, "my aunt will die."

She lit up herself, being careful to blow the smoke away from Priya. Behind her, Priya could read a billboard on the street for Lovely Fairness Crème, depicting a young woman posing with her face between her hands, over the blurb: "Lovely Fairness Crème. To make your skin Softer, Fairer . . . Naturally. In two weeks, you will be mistaken for a Ghori." Ghori, Foreigner. They of the Pale-Shades-of-Pink.

"Is that popular?" she asked, pointing.

"Oh, it's quite good," said Ashwini, one of Anu's friends. "I use it myself."

Her father's e-mails didn't stray very far from the topics Priya herself introduced; there were no searching questions, none of the curiosity she had dreaded. But yesterday he had written: Are you going to be in this weekend? I will call on (your) Sunday evening. It will be nice to hear your voice.

That, Priya knew, would be his morning. He would drink his first coffee of the day, and dial her number in India.

As though on cue, Mr. Iyer now said: "You know, I can understand your reluctance. After all, you are your father's daughter, is it not?"

Priya looked at him in complete bewilderment. "What do you mean?"

"After all, he is famous for rebelling against all these rituals. You must be knowing of the big argument he had with his parents? Your grandparents? Yes," said Mr. Iyer, "of course you are. It happened," Mr. Iyer said, "before he left for America. He liked the philosophy behind brahminism, he said, but he did not like the social rituals. He said they took certain practices beyond the realms of common sense. Your grandmother was shocked, I remember. Before he left for America, he removed his sacred thread. I believe she kept it in a box by her bed until she died. I wonder where it is now?"

Priya sat silent. Her father had never told her this story, but she knew where the thread was. It lay in a box, buried behind his dress shirts. She'd found it when she was a teenager and snooping. She'd opened it eagerly, but, unlike other neighborhood fathers who used their cupboards to hide their collections of pornography away from their prying children, all she'd found was this yellowing thread. She'd put it back in the box, unimpressed with her father's lack of imagination.

"He is still not practicing any rituals now, is he? *Poojas* and so on?"

"No," said Priya.

She was seized by a sudden, urgent curiosity.

"Okay," she said, "I'll come."

The house where the poonal ceremony was going to be held was large and rambling and yellowed, with an enormous gaily colored shamiana tent covering most of the garden. Priyamvada was dressed in a heavy silk saree that Mrs. Iyer had loaned her (and helped her put on), and she felt like a child in fancy dress.

She almost didn't recognize her.

"Anu!" Priya said in surprise. Like her, Anasuya was dressed in a silk saree, but she looked far more comfortable than Priya felt. Her long hair was neatly braided behind her head and decorated with jasmine flowers; there was no trace of the hip young woman from the café.

"So do you know the young boy who is going to participate in the ceremony?" Priya asked. And then felt remarkably foolish when Anu laughingly explained that it was her brother Mahesh.

Priya's eyes were caught by someone else from the café. Farhan, dressed in a silk kurta and pajama. She stared at him, confused.

What, he said.

"I thought, you know, I didn't expect to see . . . you know, Muslims . . ." said Priya, wishing she hadn't.

He looked irritated. "Which century are you living in?" he asked, only to answer the question himself, in a Mr. Iyer–like fashion. "Obviously the same one as my mother."

"Anyway," said Anu, "he's going to be seeing a lot more of this sort of stuff in the future."

Priya watched the smiles pass between them. "Oh," she said, "you mean, you guys are . . . ?"

"Yeah," said Anu. "We are. Except our parents don't know yet, so keep it to yourself, okay?"

"Why don't they know?" asked Priya.

"They'll probably die of shock," said Farhan. "We're still trying to figure out how to tell them. . . ."

"Write them a letter, maybe," said Anu.

"Send them a postcard," he said.

"Invite them to the wedding," said Anu. "Coming!"

She ran off towards her mother.

A poonal, or thread ceremony (Mr. Iyer had explained), was the consecration of brahminhood, the initiation to higher learning, access granted to the ancient scriptures and texts that, by equally ancient social laws, were exclusively part of the brahmin male birthright. After the ceremony, the Iyers' nephew, Mahesh, would wear his poonal, or holy thread, over his left shoulder and across his chest for the rest of his life.

The thread ceremony was to be performed in the living room, which had been cleared of all furniture. The ceremonial fire took up the center of the room, surrounded by the wooden planks that would seat Mahesh, his father, and three priests. Around them was a flower altar built from jasmine and marigolds. Rugs and mattresses on the floor provided seating for everyone else, except for the three oldest grannies, who limped their way to chairs provided especially for them. Musicians with *nadaswaram* trumpets and *tavil* drums sat on a raised dais to one side.

Priya sat down and looked around. Mrs. Iyer was engulfed by her female relatives, chatting and laughing eagerly. Mr. Iyer had joined the other menfolk. Priya didn't mind; she was absorbed in watching the faces around her, trying to imagine her young parents as part of this setting. This was the real mccoy, an indubitable passage to india, the true esmiss-esmore.

The poonal ceremony began, developing its own ancient rhythm to the chants of priests, who were dressed in white, richly bordered veshtis, chests bare, with their sacred threads over their left shoulders. Their heads were shaved, but not completely; Priya noticed that each priest had a small tuft of hair at the back of his head, a few inches long and knotted at the end. Their foreheads were painted with their caste mark: three horizontal lines in white. Her eyes wandered, mesmerized, from the priests, to the flower altar, to the floor, which was decorated with *kolam* designs, colorful and geometric, drawn by hand with rice flour. Coconuts were balanced on the narrow mouths of squat brass pots, decked with mango leaves, vermilion, and strings of jasmine flowers, next to huge silver trays laden with fruit. Every now and then the head priest would add things to the fire with his right hand: sacred reeds, ghee. Mahesh and his father, dressed in silk veshtis, sat alongside the priests around the fire. Anasuya and her mother sat close by, getting up occasionally to fetch things that the priests needed for the ceremony.

The room became warmer, with the blazing sacred fire and the collective heat of all the people crowded into that shrinking room. Women developed heat-delineated arcs under their armpits; wisps of hair escaped the fastenings of braids and top-knots, flowers and oil, to curl and frizz around their faces. The chanting seemed to get louder as the air thickened about Priya. The heat slipped under her skin: she felt the warmth rushing to her head, and descending down her brow to rest on the bridge of her nose in drops of water, thick and heavy. The cumbersome silk saree embraced her body like clingwrap.

She felt a hand on her shoulder and looked around to see Anu smiling down at her.

"Are you all right?" Anu asked. "Want something to drink?"

"I'm okay," said Priya.

"It'll be over soon," Anu whispered, squeezing her arm before moving away.

The drums and nadaswaram picked up in tempo. A white silk shawl was opened and spread over Mahesh, his father, and one of the priests. Under that protective covering, cocooned from eavesdropping ears, Priya knew, the young boy would be initiated by the priest into the ancient, secret wisdoms of brahmin-hood. When he emerged, he would officially be ready to practice Brahmacharya: to pursue knowledge with purity and devotion, to strictly eschew all sensual pleasures for the duration of his studies.

The ceremony over, the noise level rose to deafening proportions as the chatter exploded from the whispers that had earlier confined it.

Anu joined Priya. "Hi," she said. "Did you find that interesting?"

"Very," said Priya. "But tell me, isn't your brother a little too old for this? Mr. Iyer tells me it's usually done at about eight or nine years of age."

"Yes, Mahesh is twelve years old," said Anu, "and this ceremony is the result of a four-year war of attrition between him and my parents. Mahesh finally agreed, or, rather," she said, "succumbed to the bribe of a new CD player."

Mahesh's parents received everyone's congratulations, while Mahesh, under the strict supervision of an aunt, went around the room seeking the blessings of all the elders present by performing his *namaskaram,* his obeisance, before them; stretching himself out on the floor, full length, facedown, and touching his forehead to the feet of those whose blessings he sought. After about ten minutes of this, he looked a little tired. The route to a CD player was long and hard.

"So," Anasuya said. "My brother is a Brahmin. And tomorrow he will no doubt celebrate by eating a beef burger."

"Did you have to go through this, too?"

"Oh no," said Anu. "This is strictly a male thing. Come for lunch."

Lunch was served under the big tent in the garden, and eaten off banana leaves laid on long trestle tables. Priyamvada found herself seated next to Anu and Farhan. She watched what other people did, and tried to imitate them. The guests seated themselves and washed the big banana leaves by ceremonially pouring water from the water tumblers into their cupped right hands and sprinkling it over the leaves. Then the caterers, who had been cooking all morning in the backyard, walked quickly through with their big buckets of vegetarian food, precisely ladling each item onto its prescribed location on the banana leaf—a place for everything and everything in its place: salt, pickle, sweet, relish, *papad, vada,* varieties of vegetable *poriyal* and *aviyal*—twelve different types of side dishes altogether, and, finally, steaming mounds of rice. Plain rice served with ghee and lentil *sambar;* ghee and spicy, watery rasam. Lemon rice. Coconut rice. Tamarind rice. Curd rice. All of it followed by huge servings of sweet jaggery-and-coconut-flavored milk *payasam.*

"Where," whispered Farhan, "are the fucking chicken kebabs?"

"Shh," said Anasuya. "Someone will hear you."

Priya had read somewhere that, in India, table manners while eating with the hand stressed not dirtying more than the tips of one's fingers. This was a text that a lot of the poonal guests were apparently not familiar with. Their right hands surrounded the mounds of rice on the banana leaves, squeezing and squashing until the glutinous rice emerged in pasty white tendrils from the gaps between the fingers. The rice was then mixed with sambar and rolled into a ball before being tossed into the mouth and masticated in an enthusiastic dance of teeth and tongue.

Priya wondered if she should ask for a spoon, but only for a moment. This was clearly a moment to Act Local, but not Think Global. She placed her right hand over the rice and squeezed, feeling like a child allowed to play, messily, squashily, happily.

She found herself asking Farhan: "Would you like to leave all this and live in America?"

"No, but I can see why your parents would," he said, answering the question in her mind. "Things were different for them. Today, I can work in the same firm as your father, without leaving India. He couldn't. Things are different. We have choices now."

Choice. It was her father's word, one he used whenever Priya pressed him for an explanation of why he came to America. "Choice," he would say, which Priya had always assumed was his own particular synonym for "Money."

After lunch, Priya waited for Mrs. Iyer to say good-bye. She clutched a bag that had been offered as the parting gift to all guests. It contained all manner of propitious things: a coconut, two betel leaves, packets of red *kumkum* and turmeric powders, an *elakki* banana. And, with it, a small silver coin as a memento of the occasion, and a small bunch of jasmine and frangipani flowers strung together. Anasuya joined her again. Farhan had left, discreetly, with other guests.

"Would you like a *paan?*"

Anu's mother was seated on the verandah, rolling paan for everybody: spreading the betel leaves with chalky white *chunam*, tucking in the crushed betel nuts, and rolling up the leaves in a swift gesture that was born of long practice. "You may not like it," said Anu. "It is very bitter. But if you chew it long enough, it will stain your mouth a bright, lovely red."

They strolled about the grounds together, chewing paan, and made their way over to where Mahesh was, on the far side of the verandah. He looked miserable and bored, ensconced with the priest whose business it was to teach him the sacred Gayatri Mantra. He stuck his tongue out at Anasuya, and turned his attention back to the priest, who was by now looking almost as desperate as Mahesh.

"It'll come, boy. It'll come," he told Mahesh in Tamil. "Repeat after me, one more time . . . *Om bhoor bhuvah suvaha . . .*"

The Gayatri Mantra had first been whispered into Mahesh's ear under the protection of the ceremonial shawl. Priya listened, and then turned to Anu.

"So, you don't know this mantra, right? Since it's only for brahmin males?"

Anu laughed, and recited, without pause.

> *Om Bhoor Bhuvah Suvaha*
> *Tat Savitr-varenyam*
> *Bhargo Devasya Dheemahee*
> *Dhiyoyonah Prachodayat*
>
> *O supreme brahman, earth, universe, and heavens,*
> *O sun, supreme brahman, source of all creation*
>   *manifested,*
> *Supreme enlightened of all celestial energies,*
> *Let my intellect be ignited*

"My uncle taught it to me," Anasuya said. "A very long time ago.

"Mr. Iyer," she explained, in response to Priyamvada's look of inquiry.

"Oh," said Priya.

She waved good-bye and walked to the car, the sonorous Sanskrit verse still singing in her ears with the sweetness of a stolen secret.

Priyamvada returned from the poonal ceremony and sat before the computer. Her hand halted on the keys.

His last e-mail said: We are missing you. When do you plan to return?

The night before her departure, he had wandered into her room and said: Look, why don't you just go and see the Taj Mahal and have a good time?

His tone was conciliatory, but Priya had been insulted.

She had lectured him, and then swore that if things didn't go as she'd anticipated she would eat her hat, or rather, seriously consider any career choices he might suggest. Even if this meant her suiting up and going to work in a corporation that worshipped greed and destroyed the environment and spread American pop culture like a disease through the world.

Now, with hands poised on the keyboard, what she wanted to say to her father was an inchoate jumble of thoughts, all bumping into each other: Do you know the Gayatri Mantra? she could ask. It is so beautiful, so powerful. I heard it from Anu—right after she told me the problems that she and Farhan would face with their respective families. And that is India, she could say, segueing into a lecture—divisive, a maddening mixture of ancient values and modern pop culture, of great wisdoms and blank ignorance.

Or she could simply shut up, say nothing, go quietly to see the Taj Mahal, have a drunken good time and then, heading home, offer to report for work in a corporation of his choice. Though, with sudden insight, she knew that he would not really ask it of her. He would continue, as he had always done, to let her find her own path.

Or she could just spit it out, say-it-loud say-it-proud, put the words on the screen in bold black on white and send them off to him: I can see why you made the choices you did, and I thank you for allowing me to make my own.

Her hands remained still and silent. She switched off the computer and covered it carefully with the plastic sheets. She glanced at her watch. In a very short while it would be evening in India and morning in America, and her father would reach for the telephone. And she would discover whether she had the courage to say to him, in person, what she couldn't bring herself to write.

On the verandah, Mr. Iyer was poring through a reference book. "We are," he said, "in a very modern city." He handed the book to her.

The Limca Book of Records, it said on the cover. It had all sorts of rankings inside. Bangalore, Priyamvada learned, had the first online retailer in India. It had India's first oxygen bar and largest wine-and-cheese shop. The Cyber Crime Police Station was the first in the country to solve any sort of cyber crime. Bangalore was also the first Indian city to hold a Biotechnology Quiz, and was home to the first-ever Indian Institute of Cartoonists.

"Is it not impressive?" Mr. Iyer beamed. And then he asked: "You are enjoying your trip?"

Yes, he said, I can see you are.

MYSORE
COFFEE

The socialite in Delhi jumped from the hotel roof on Tuesday night.

She fell a hundred feet to a smooth tiled floor lined with flowerpots. The socialite was related by blood and marriage to some very prominent political and arms-dealing families, which (some people said) were one and the same thing, and the pictures of the suicide were on the front pages of all the newspapers.

Sita saw the news with her morning coffee. She read it from beginning to end and then she tore the article out of the paper, tucked it into her briefcase, and carried it with her to work.

By the end of the week, Sita had built up quite a collection of news scraps, with photographs of the socialite and articles that focused on the day of her death, as though that were the important thing and not all the days that preceded it.

Sita had never met the socialite in Delhi.

To be perfectly honest, she had never heard of her before her suicide. Over this week, of course, Sita felt that she had come to know her quite well. She could recite, from memory, where the socialite went to college, the names of her children, and where she liked to lunch. She repeated the information to herself at odd moments, and scanned the news every day for more.

The office is humming, as it usually does on a weekday morning. The décor is standard-issue open plan, the low-walled cubicles sown with men in ties and women in sarees and pretty secretaries all in a row.

Sita avoids all conversation.

Instead, she forces her attention to the financial spreadsheet on the computer screen. SigmaSoft, it says in the heading. It is the in-depth analysis of a client's accounts, which has taken her days to complete. She usually enjoys this part of her work, there is a satisfaction to stacking the numbers neatly, and watching the columns balance out at the end. Assets greater than Liabilities equals Positive Shareholders Equity. There is an even greater pleasure in playing with the numbers on her screen, running calculations of financial ratios to determine short-term liquidity and the rate of return on assets. These are the magic spells of her world, incantations that reveal the truth about everything.

The numbers never lie.

She has worked hard at it, but today she scrolls through the document, apathy swirling through the edges of her brain. She vaguely considers calling in sick, but only for a moment. The idea of staying at home, with her mother hovering solicitously, curiously, apprehensively, around her, is even less appealing.

Better to stay hidden behind her computer and just let the day drift to an end.

"Hi, Sita." Ramu makes his way to her desk and props himself against the side of the table. Sita can feel her face begin to flush.

Ramu is handsome, with laughing eyes. He is handsome, and discussing work is the only way that Sita knows to have a conversation with him.

"Listen," he says. "I want to be able to work together with you on this," he says. "Okay?"

Sita stares back at him. His face is leaning into hers, so close that his features dissolve into separate parts. His nose, slightly hooked, separating eyes rendered even darker by their intensity, placed under well-defined brows. The neatly trimmed goatee resting on his chin. His mouth, stretching into a smile, speaking words that take a long time to reach her ears. The expensive shirt and carefully coordinated tie that encase his neck.

She can smell his cologne, long after he walks away from her.

She tries to read the numbers on the screen. Her hand travels over her head, locating the stray hairs that are uncurling, one by one, from the tight thick braid. She has forgotten to apply the coconut oil that keeps her hair smooth and shiny, braided and quiescent. Behind her back, her hair slyly attempts to break free.

No, it is no good.

The restlessness in her mind has seized her body. It is fidgety, unhappy. It wishes to slap at the air around her, tear her braid loose, rip her clothes off one by one, and laugh and weep.

She tells her office that she has work at the Registrar of Companies and walks to the exit. She passes Ramu's desk. He is seated at a cubicle similar to hers, but with the air of someone who is confident of moving into one of the glass-encased offices, reserved for senior management, that line the windows. As she walks by, he is scrolling through his computer screen and flipping through a document on his desk while talking into the telephone cradled on his shoulder.

Godlike multihanded activity managed with élan.

Sita glances at her watch and knows, instinctively, that Ramu is talking to someone in America. Someone, she knows, who will not let the fact that it is late at night in America prevent them from discussing the work ahead, or from laughing joyously at the slightest joke.

As she walks by, Ramu looks up and winks.

Sita goes to her car and wonders where to go, what to do.

The socialite in Delhi on her last day did a great many things. She woke up, as she usually did, at noon, and drank some freshly squeezed carrot juice. She then dressed herself in Prada jeans and an embroidered vest from Rajasthan (she was famous for the mixing of traditional and trendy) and went out to lunch at the stylish new restaurant Monsoon Orange with her best friends, Mimsy Kumar and Pinky Chawla. She ate a large green salad, tossed with sun-dried tomatoes, olives, and a lemongrass vinaigrette. The socialite, who was fastidious about her health and appearance, didn't eat any of the desserts that the restaurant was famous for. Instead she ordered french-pressed Java coffee, which she drank black, with no sugar. After lunch she shopped, returned home, played with her children for a little while, and got ready to go to a party. The newspapers carried photographs of that party, held in a five-star luxury hotel.

Six hours later, she climbed to the roof of the hotel, and jumped.

Driving usually soothes Sita, steadies her, helps her focus.

She likes the disorder on the roads, it binds all the crazed vehicles together as they rush about, cars, scooters, buses, trucks, skipping schoolboy pedestrians, wandering cows, bicycles, bullock carts; honking and cutting through traffic lanes as they speed to offices, to shops, to homes, to schools, to various government jobs in the sewage and electricity boards—where, naturally, the whole thing, the urgency, the rush at the traffic lights, the life-or-death driving, the swerves and near misses, the almost-airdashes, comes to a crashing halt and time slows down, time catches its breath, time covers its face with a hanky and goes to sleep, only to wake up peevishly complaining about the tedious inefficiencies of the water and electric supply and the general breakdown of social discipline.

Usually, Sita is an active part of the chaos on the roads, but not today.

This morning, she is paralyzed. The traffic flows around her, cutting into and out of her lane, scowling faces darting angry looks at her through windows flashing past. The air-conditioning inside hums softly. She bought the car after her last promotion. It is new, glossy, and will take five years to pay off. Behind the wheel, Sita can feel the pinch of her bra tighten around her, a line of sweat that digs into her lungs, squeezing her breath and marking the skin below in red lines that will take a day to fade.

The previous night, Sita stayed late at work and, ignoring the computer spreadsheets she was supposed to be working on, started searching the Internet instead. There were seventy-eight thousand results for the phrase "suicide hotline." She chose one at random and clicked on the link. She was immediately led to a page that was colored in serious black, with the message IF YOU ARE THINKING OF COMMITTING SUICIDE, READ THIS NOW pasted at the top, with the words "suicide" and "now" picked out in bright bloody red. Sita did as they suggested and read the page through. Just give me five minutes, the writer urged. Five minutes to explain how suicide can seem like a solution when the mental pain you feel exceeds your abilities to cope with that pain. Or rather (with mathematical elegance) how

Pain greater than Pain-Coping Resources equals Suicide.

Or rather, when grief and anguish build and build, layer upon layer, within the mind, without relief, ceaselessly, even while you smile and laugh and act so normal that people later look at each other in complete surprise and disbelief.

This was presumably what happened to the Delhi socialite.

And what had happened, twenty-three years earlier, to Sita's father.

When she was young, they told her that her father had been killed on the way home from the barbershop. This scene had played itself over and over in Sita's mind. Her father, hair neatly trimmed, odd remnants of it still clinging, dustlike, to his white shirt, climbing onto his scooter and weaving his way home, behind a truck that failed to heed the squeak of the scooter horn and turned suddenly to the right. He'd had no choice, they told her, but to cleave right into it, killing himself instantly. Sita could imagine it happening: the traffic swirling around his fallen body in baffling patterns, accompanied by the squeal of horns and the shouts of drivers.

Even now, there was a part of her that was reluctant to give up her father's accident; it was a truth embedded deep within herself. Even now, she found herself telling strangers that, yes, my father died in a traffic accident. Yes, so terrible, I know.

But of course, that was a lie.

Twenty-three years earlier, Bangalore had been a very flat city. The highest one could go was perhaps three stories in the saree arcade on JC Road. And then, things changed. Overnight, some tall buildings began to appear. The Unity Building was the tallest on Mahatma Gandhi Road, and then came the flats built by the Mysore Builders on Cunningham Road. People went to look at them, to marvel and to feel proud. Skyscrapers meant that the city was, finally, growing up. When the third building went up, the Palace Towers (also on MG Road), it was said to be the prettiest of all, a full ten stories high, and covered with sandstone.

Sita went with her parents to see. They climbed to the top, and Sita's mother peeped over the edge, holding her husband's shirtsleeve with one hand. "Giddy!" she giggled, and wouldn't let Sita take a peek. They went down, stopping at the vendor to buy hot corn roasted over charcoal and smeared with lime and green mint chutney, perfect for the chill post-monsoon winds of September.

Her father stared up at the building, which towered over them. "Looks like your father's nose," he said to his wife, who didn't frown as she usually might at such a comment. She giggled again, her laughter contagious. Sita remembered laughing herself, and seeing her father do the same. They finished their corn and went home, Sita's father driving the scooter, her mother daintily sitting sideways on the seat behind him, one hand wrapped protectively around her daughter, who was placed between them, sandwiched snugly by the warmth of her parents' bodies as she gazed at the world that flashed by.

The next day, her father came back by himself, climbed his father-in-law's nose, and threw himself over.

The building was still there. Tall, covered in sandstone. Sita had avoided it for twenty-three years. But earlier this week she rode the elevator to the terrace and stayed there for two hours. She did not really have any choice in the matter. On Tuesday night, her boss took his entire team to Palace Towers to eat.

"The new restaurant there is supposed to be very good," he said. "And the views are fantastic." Everyone in the office was pleased; this was a reward for work well done. They arrived as a group, six men, three women. They parked the two cars that had brought them in the basement, and clustered together inside the elevator that sped right to the top. Half the restaurant was enclosed in air-conditioning, the other half spread out over the terrace, with tables dressed in yellow-checked tablecloths and candlelight and vibrant with blue and orange crockery. Their boss said, "I love trying out new restaurants. Especially when there is such a good view," and Sita had watched him stand near the railing and gaze at the twinkling lights of the city.

She had prepared her mind for North Indian food, dishes like chicken tikka and tandoori fish and mutton biriyani, or, in her case, their vegetarian equivalents, loaded with the garlic and spices her traditional Tamil brahmin mother never used. Instead the menu card was full of Western dishes that Sita spelled her way through, unsure of what they were and how to pronounce them. She heard Ramu say, "The bouillabaisse sounds good . . ." and her boss reply, "Mm, yes. And the chicken tagliatelle."

The conversation grew animated, cheery, the laughter moving freely back and forth. Sita sat quietly, with the force of long habit. It had always been so with her. The confidence she felt in analyzing her spreadsheets eroded when she was face-to-face with clients or in meetings—the words of explanation that leaped to her mouth fading away. She was used to seeing the fruit of her work being usurped by noisier, louder colleagues who knew less than her but who were better with words, and who seemed to thrive in an environment that placed undue value on the glossiness of their hair, the crispness of their attire, and the smoothness of their speech.

"Do you like this restaurant, Sita," her boss asked her heartily. "I remember when this building was first built," he said. "God, Bangalore was an entirely different city in those days. No traffic, so peaceful. You were probably too young to remember it."

Sita smiled mutely. On the other side of the building lay the speckled mosaic floor, a hundred feet down, unchanged after twenty-three years, spattered with the inlaid spots that still contained traces of her father, his smile, the feel of his hand resting on her shoulder, captured and imprisoned along with her mother's laughter.

Her father had been an accountant like herself, working in a small office of six people. He made a mistake, one day. It was an honest mistake, but one that unfortunately could not be corrected in time. It cost the client an additional four thousand rupees in taxes. Such a silly, small amount of money. Four months of her father's salary, then. Today, no more than a single monthly installment on Sita's car loan, or the cost of dinner on Tuesday night for nine people at the new restaurant.

Her father checked his bank account, left the five hundred rupees in it untouched, and took his wife and daughter to see the new skyscraper on Mahatma Gandhi Road.

When she received the office memo about the Tuesday dinner program, Sita panicked at first, and toyed with the idea of telephoning Christine in America and asking her what she should do. But she didn't. She already knew what her friend's advice would be.

"Just say no," Christine would say, pulling an appropriate Americanism out of the air. "Tell them to take a walk. Put your foot down. Stand up for yourself."

But these things were beyond Sita.

She knew, too, that it wasn't something she could discuss with her mother, before or after the event. "How could you?" her mother would ask, shocked, sorrowed; and Sita would have to admit: with great difficulty. Her mother would say no more about it, at least not during the day. Instead it would manifest itself in the middle of the night, which was when Sita's mother usually battled with the ghosts of her mind, waking up, ghoul-like, tormented, weeping into her pillow, a low keening sound that, through the years, had pulled Sita from her own bed to sit by her mother's side, to hold her hand and pat her back until the

sobs died down. Her mother's cheerful daytime energy never reflected the anguish of the preceding night, but she told Sita, frequently and tenderly: Oh, you are a good daughter. What would
my life be without you?

Christine would have said that Sita's mother had never
learned to let go.

Christine, who was the very opposite of Sita's mother, and
clung to her work with a fierce determination, while sliding easily in and out of human relationships.

Their first contact had been through e-mail. Forwarded to her by
her boss, it was from an American company looking for investment opportunities in India. It was brisk and businesslike, and
signed, at the bottom, Best regards, Christine Miller, Associate
Vice President. "Look into it," her boss said, and so Sita dutifully
wrote back, enclosing a list of deals that her firm had concluded
in recent times, signing her letter, Yours sincerely, Sita Ranganathan, Manager. In the second e-mail, Christine addressed
her breezily: Dear Sita, she said, immediately on first-name
terms. And, surprised by her own insouciance, Sita wrote back:
Dear Christine.

They met, finally, two months and many e-mails later. Christine arrived for a visit to Bangalore, to see for herself if any of
the investment ideas identified by Sita's firm were satisfactory.
Sita dressed herself carefully that day, in a silk saree, her wavy
hair carefully oiled and braided and lying thick and heavy along
her spine. She waited eagerly in the office lobby for the car to arrive, and almost quailed when she saw the woman in the dark
blue suit emerge. Christine stood eight inches taller than Sita,

teutonic, pale, with short blond hair, blue eyes, and a loud, ac-
cented voice that made people turn around and stare. "Hi!" she
said. "Sita? Great to finally meet you!" Sita smiled tentatively, and
was delighted, so relieved, to see Christine smile eagerly back.

In the office, Ramu sized Christine up from a distance and
said: "*Arrey,* bedding a woman that size would be like sleeping
with a gorilla." During the meeting that followed, however, she
noticed that he was very courteous, chatting easily with Christine about places in America he'd visited on holiday and, later,
the merits of her company's proposed investments.

It was a fact, Sita knew, that this project was never meant to
develop into anything quite so big. It was why, Sita knew, she was
given the task in the first place. It was supposed to be small, lead-
ing nowhere, and when it grew, no one, least of all her boss,
knew how to get Sita off the project. But then, as days went by, as
Christine freely praised Sita's work in e-mails that were forwarded through the office, her boss began to look at her differ-
ently. He leaned forward now when she opened her mouth.
Finally, as a vote of confidence, he suggested: So, Sita, why don't
you go to America and meet the team there? Go see their factories. Give me a report.

Everyone else in the office stared, and Ramu lounged across
her desk later that day, chatting lightly of this and that, as though
she were somebody else.

The following weekend, Sita went out and bought her new
car, the biggest extravagance of her whole life.

In the Palace Towers restaurant on Tuesday night, her boss
ordered mozzarella sticks and onion rings as snacks. Sita

remembered the onion rings from her trip to America, but the mozzarella sticks were new to her. She watched the others help themselves to the fried cheese and accompanying sauce, and copied them.

The restaurant became crowded, with fashionably dressed people filling the other tables. Her boss, and Ramu, and a couple of others at her table, seemed to know some of the other guests, but Sita recognized no one.

"Hi, Ramu," a woman waved from across the room. He looked around and grinned; the two women with her waved and smiled also.

"I say, Ramu," their boss said appreciatively, "ladies' man, is it?"

"Isn't that Ashwini?" someone asked at their table. Sita said nothing in reply.

She always knew, instinctively, what he thought of her. She was what men like Ramu called *"pavam."* Literally, poor thing. Metaphorically, something worse than the pity those words automatically evoked. Something un-chic, old-fashioned, timid. No fun at all. To be avoided at all costs, except in the line of duty.

The socialite in Delhi didn't look pavam. She looked very chic indeed. The newspaper carried before and after pictures of her, alive before and dead after, as though covering the effects of some weight loss or beauty treatment. In the before, the socialite looked beautiful. She was dressed casually, in tight jeans and a tank top that rested lightly on her slim shoulders, a cigarette held carelessly in her fingers. She was laughing into the camera, her fashionably layered and straightened hair falling slightly across her face, her mouth outlined in some subtle, lip-plumping shade of lipstick and parted to reveal her seed-pearl teeth. Her eyes

were her strongest feature, large, a lustrous deep brown, under
the arches of her delicately plucked black eyebrows, winging
their way upward to her temples. After seeing that photograph,
Sita went to the beauty parlor to have her own eyebrows shaped.
When it was done, she looked at herself in the mirror and knew
that it was a mistake. She didn't look chic, she looked cheap.
Cheap in the manner of the Tamil movie actresses that her
mother despised, with their faces artificially brightened and colored, and the plumpness of their bodies barely concealed by the
too-tight blouses and transparent sarees that revealed cleavage
and belly button trembling to the sound of the music and the
lust in the hero's eyes.

In America, she and Christine had driven through miles of country, on a road trip that took them through almost ten factories
and offices. During the day, they lunched on the road, quickly
and efficiently; in the evenings, they dined lavishly at company
expense. Christine would order whisky and wine, while Sita
sipped soft drinks and, for the first time in her life, didn't feel the
least bit pavam. For Christine, Sita knew, this friendship was special, but then Christine had many special friends. For Sita, Christine was fast becoming the first real friend she had ever had. She
wanted to tell her this, but never could bring herself to actually
say the words. Instead, their dinnertime conversation revolved
easily and lightly around deals they had done, and in Christine's
case, her family and friends and men she had slept with. She
laughed loudly, and Sita laughed with her.

Occasionally Christine would interrupt the meal to deal with
some personal matter, casually and briskly. "Sure," she would say

into the cell phone. "I'll swing by. I'm busy now, but maybe next weekend? My mother," she'd explain to Sita, "she's broken her ankle. She's in this retirement facility—they take really good care of her, but I bet she drives them crazy." And in response to Sita's wondering question: "Sure, we get along fine. Though she can be a real bitch sometimes." And the bubbles from the soft drink would slide up Sita's nose in shock.

Or she would jettison a lover, Christine would, with the same smile that had probably tempted them there in the first place, and that perhaps kept them from feeling any rancor when she said good-bye. "Take care of yourself. You're worth it," she would say, blowing kisses into the telephone. "You're wonderful. Good-bye." And then she would order another drink and start talking about someone else.

Sita knew herself to be a good daughter; this is so *wrong,* she would think as she listened to Christine, only to find herself smiling back across the table. She tried to imagine herself saying similar things, about Ramu perhaps, carelessly: Oh yeah, I slept with him because he was a good kisser; but jeez, he was a lot better up *here* than he was down *there*.

But one night she did talk about a man: Sita talked about her father and the road accident that had killed him. Halfway through, tempted by the sympathy in Christine's eyes, she stopped and cleared her throat and started the story afresh. This time the truth, his suicide. Christine had listened, her eyes filling with tears. Christ, Sita, she'd said. Christ.

Sita returned from America with a clarity about Christine's firm and their requirements that her previous, long-distance analysis had never been able to achieve. Their interest lay in software development; they wanted to acquire an established player; and Sita soon located a company that might be a good match. She had met one of the owners of this company, SigmaSoft, at a conference; she knew they would be willing to sell. Sita pored through their dossier and spent the entire weekend quietly by herself on the computer. She entered the figures into her spreadsheet, her fingers moving swiftly across the number pad, her mind processing the information in front of her, moving through ideas for restructuring the business in a way that would make the acquisition viable. By Tuesday afternoon she knew the deed could be done. She felt like picking up the phone and calling Christine immediately. She knew how the conversation would go: she would state her information, Christine would cheer and say something like, fucking hell, Sita, that's great. Awesome.

Before she could do that, however, she first needed to run it by her boss. They were all supposed to go out to the Palace Towers restaurant that night, and, for the first time since her boss had brought it up, Sita thought that she might actually be able to go through with it. Dinner tonight at the restaurant, a meeting with her boss tomorrow morning. This time, she promised herself, she would do it properly. Take a leaf out of Christine's book, Ramu's book, speak with confidence and strength.

He wandered by her desk later that day.

"Hey," Ramu said casually. "What's up?" "Nothing," she said, as usual. And then she found herself saying, "Actually." An inner excitement was urging her to preen, for the first time. Ramu caught the animation on her face and raised his eyebrows, smiling. She pulled out the hard copies of the spreadsheets she had so carefully worked on and handed them to him. "That's *fantastic*," Ramu said, and she saw admiration warm his eyes, and heat her skin.

The bread-coated cheese served in the Palace Towers restaurant that night tasted rubbery and salty in Sita's mouth, even after she coated it in sauce and took a second nibble.

"Try the onion rings," Ramu said from across the table.

She found herself smiling back at him without averting her eyes.

"So, Sita," her boss said, contravening his own rules about not discussing work at the restaurant. "How are things going on that account? That America trip of yours was useful?"

Sita could feel the heat rise within her as everyone turned to look at her. This was not the forum in which she had anticipated discussing her ideas. Her teeth had closed around an onion ring, grabbing and dragging the slippery vegetable out of its casing. She tried to stuff it into her mouth. Her eyes swiveled helplessly to Ramu.

He leaned forward and addressed the table. "I personally think," he said, "that SigmaSoft would be a good match."

Sita felt her throat clench, gagging over the onion ring, blocking the words that rose hastily within her. By the time she swallowed her mouthful, Ramu had explained all her ideas, the business restructuring, the possible acquisition value, everything.

She heard her boss say: "That's fantastic, Ramu."

Then he said: "Isn't it?" And everyone else agreed.

The women from the neighboring table finished their meal

and stopped to say good-bye on their way out. The one called Ashwini put her hands on Ramu's shoulders. "Call me," she said.

The next morning, the newspapers were full of the socialite's suicide the night before in Delhi.

Sita rushed to the office, but Ramu had got there first.

"Sita," her boss said when she walked in. "I know you will agree with me on this. I think it might be best if we put Ramu in charge of this account. What do you say?"

And once again, Ramu stole her words from her. "I have to say," he said, holding her gaze, "that Sita really contributed. I mean, really, the whole thing was her idea."

Her boss smiled, pleased at this demonstration of Ramu's modesty and teamwork. Good, good, he said. She, too, shall work with you on this. But you take the lead.

The next day, towards evening, Sita received a phone call from Christine, who'd been shocked to hear about the change of guard. "That's terrible," Christine said. "You were doing such a great job." Something professional seemed to slide through her voice. "Look after yourself, okay?" Christine said. "You deserve it. You're wonderful."

A few months earlier, Sita had visited one of those new department stores in the city that market Western lifestyles to Indian homes that were previously starved of wineglasses and aromatherapy candles and Provençal-inspired dishes. She was with Christine, who, with American efficiency, was trying to squeeze in a Saturday morning's worth of shopping on an otherwise whistle-stop business trip through Bangalore. Christine wanted to shop for mementos, but not, she was explaining, for something Provençal; where was the brass and incense-sticks, she wanted to know. Next stop, Sita said, and returned to contemplating the items on display.

The candles set in holders that let the beholders think on, meditate, on their ability to imitate . . . The music changed, and Sita's feet began to tap while, next to her, Christine's feet came to a complete halt. Sita looked up to see her consternation.

"I can't believe they're playing this . . ." said Christine. Eminem. Eminem! Who the fuck would confuse the fucking *anger* in his voice, she said, with easy listening?

Sita listened to the voice saying, Working at Burger King, Spitting on your Onion Rings. It's American, she explained. Creates the right atmosphere. Good rhythm.

But the lyrics. The fucking lyrics. Aren't people offended?

I don't think it matters, Sita said. As long as it sounds American and popular.

Don't tell me, said Christine, that people cannot distinguish between *this* song and the Billy fucking *Joel* that was playing earlier?

Well, you know those Americans, Sita said. They all sound alike.

After that final telephone conversation with Christine, Sita stayed behind after almost everyone else had left. The office was quiet, pooled in darkness, half the lights switched off except for her corner, which was brightly lit, and another one further down. Sita found herself avoiding her spreadsheets and surfing the Internet. She felt strangely reluctant to leave the office, held in her seat by Ramu's presence. He was waiting, in his turn, to receive a conference call from America, from Christine and the rest of her team.

Her ears heard every move he made, the squeak of his chair as he pushed it back, the gluck-gluck of the water as it spilled down his throat. The sound of the bottle being replaced on the table. She had a similar bottle on hers. A glass one that she kept filled with water from the cooler at the other end of the office. It glistened now, the bottle, catching the overhead light. It glistened maliciously, seeming to taunt her.

He was talking into his cell phone. "Let's meet for a drink," he was saying, to one of those women from the restaurant, or perhaps someone who looked like them. His head was turned away from her.

What if she picked up the glass bottle that stood on her table and brought it down upon that neat and glossy head of hair? Did it once, and then again and again until the water mingled with his blood and he lay imprisoned in the floor beneath her feet?

Her fingers moved of their own volition; they curled tightly around the narrow mouth of the bottle. She lifted her hand and, with the exhilaration of a music conductor waving a baton, brought the bottle down against the side of her table. The glass shattered and curved like a scattered wave over the floor, the water puddled at her feet, her hand dropped the remaining piece as the tremendous sound of the crash washed through her shocked body.

"Oh my god. What happened?"

She could see Ramu peering in her direction. She could see him move towards her, his face registering curiosity, then amazement, as he absorbed the tears that were spilling out of her eyes, and the blood that seeped from her fingers.

He pulled out a starched white handkerchief from his pocket. "Take it easy, butterfingers," he said, and wrapped it carefully around her hand. "There." He smiled down at her.

"Do you think you'll be able to give me the SigmaSoft spreadsheets by tomorrow?" he asked.

The writer on the Internet suicide hotline suggested that, in times of Pain, it is wise to increase one's Pain-Coping Resources. Accordingly, Sita went home that night and, over dinner, told her mother everything. Her work. Christine. Ramu. Her mother's eyes were gentle with sympathy and comfort. She listened and spooned food onto Sita's plate and urged her to eat. And even as she felt the soothing solace of her mother's concern, Sita wondered what her father would have said. Stand up and fight, or flee, flee, flee. Flee this earth and hope for better luck next time.

She woke up in the middle of the night, the darkness of her dreams still upon her.

She could hear her mother crying in the room next door. She felt herself falter. She was too full of her own emotion to try and absorb any more. But her mother's tears did not stop. Sita got out of bed.

"Oh," said her mother, "I thought perhaps you had decided not to come."

I'm here, I'm here, Sita murmured, and patted her mother on her back.

"Who do I have? Tell me that? In my troubles, who is there to stand beside me and help?" Her mother's voice broke in the dark, heavy with tears.

I am here, Ma, I am here.

No, said her mother. You are not. You heard me crying, and yet you paused before you came. You are in your own misery, over that boy.

What, you think he is going to marry you?

Who will touch you, with your family's stigma? Do you think of that? Did your father think of that? He took his life, and our life with it, yours and mine. Did he think? No, even in death, he was selfish.

You are becoming like him. You were there for me once, but no more. Well, go from here.

Go. Go! Get out of this room. Your father got out, didn't he? Well, you get out too.

But Sita stayed, holding her mother's hand. She said nothing, the water draining silently out of her eyes and down her cheeks. Her mother finally fell into exhausted sleep, and Sita went out to the living room. She sat on her father's favorite rosewood chair, feeling the weight of the air upon her body, pressing down on her face, sinking like lead into her lungs, pushing her arms and legs into the hard wood beneath. Her fingers splayed stiffly against her leg, unbendable. The room was freezing.

Her mother shook her gently awake the next morning. "*Kanna,*" she said. "Darling. Want some coffee?"

As she had for the past three days, Sita studied the newspapers for stories of the socialite, feeling a strange yearning in her blood.

★ ★ ★

Now Sita finds herself directing the car to Palace Towers. There is a fragility to her body, as though all the pieces of it are being held together by willpower alone. She parks the car, squeezing it between two others, and climbs out. She stumbles slightly over the broken pavement, and water sparks unreasonably in her eyes. The watchman hands her a little yellow parking receipt, and she digs in her handbag for twenty rupees. "You can pay later," he says. "That's okay," she says.

The lift is empty of all save the lift-boy. "The restaurant is closed," he tells her. "Not open for lunch, only dinner. But the coffee shop is open."

That's okay, she tells him.

The socialite jumped in the middle of the night. Some people said she jumped stone-cold sober, without a whimper, flying through the air like a fashion fairy, borne on wings of dark despair. Others said, no, she drank herself into a stupor and simply stepped off the roof when she could drink no more. In the after pictures, her face was unrecognizable; bruised and swollen and blackened with pain.

Sita sometimes wondered what led the socialite to choose this particular method—had she thought about alternatives? A sharp razor aimed at her wrists, slicing neatly into the flesh the way meat-eaters sliced into their food; or, perhaps, the uncomfortable swallowing of many pills? What about picking up a knife and plunging it with full force into the stomach? Or driving a car superfast right into a joyfully welcoming tree. Finding a gun

amongst her family's gun-running resources, and pointing it at
herself, staring at her triumphant reflection in the mirror right up
to that last moment when it is obscured by flying flecks of blood.
Or that culturally preferred Indian manner of self-immolation,
revered by myth, of drenching one's clothes with fuel and then
lighting a match, allowing the quick-jumping flame to dance
lightly over the body. Why jump from a tall building? Sita has
imagined it repeatedly: the wind blowing stiffly, lightly drying the
wetness on the cheeks, the slight sense of vertigo; the fascinating
pull of the earth far below, and the wondrous comfort that the
next time she touches that earth, all the pain will be gone.

The coffee shop is one floor below the restaurant. Sita enters it
on sudden impulse. It is part of a new chain that is sweeping
through the city, all brass and glass and air-conditioning, a sterile
antidote to the potholed dust and noise of the street below. Sita
reads the menu of coffees available, pausing over each one. The
socialite in Delhi drank a cup of french-pressed Java coffee the
day she died. This is also the same coffee that Christine prefers.
Sita hesitates, and then orders the same thing.

The coffee scalds her lips when it arrives and she sets the plastic cup down in a hurry. The brew seems too black, too thin, too
foreign for her taste. Her mouth is trained to the traditional
Mysore coffee prepared every single morning by her mother:
wake up before sunrise, roast and grind the beans, and filter
them through the compact steel decoction maker until the coffee flows thick and dark and strong. Temper with the bitterness
and sorrow of a lifetime and mix with freshly boiled, steaming

hot milk that has the cream frothing on the top. Add sugar and serve in tall steel tumblers, resting in flat-bottomed steel bowls, or *davaras*. That is the coffee that flows in Sita's veins. But in these newfangled coffeehouses, all you get are weak-kneed innovations: café americano, café mocha, café latte. Sita cautiously adds a bit of milk and tries again. Sticking out her tongue, dipping it into the fragrant liquid, waiting for the alien flavors to climb gently into her mouth.

At a very early age, Sita understood that her father's death had somehow set her and her mother apart—divorced from friends, and later, from suitors; bound together, her mother and herself, to each other, in a separate universe. Her mother has always maintained that, between the two of them, they could get through almost anything, and for a long time Sita carried that hope within her like a talisman.

Now she suddenly wonders if her mother had ever said that to her father as well.

She feels herself beginning to shake. She abandons her coffee and leaves the coffee shop. The staircase is hidden next to the elevator. She walks up to the next level; it is deserted, the restaurant is closed. The balcony next to the restaurant looks out over the central atrium of the building, which soars lavishly to the roof.

Sita balances her hands on the railing and stares at the mosaic floor ten stories below. Seductive, compelling, it beckons to her.

Once more, she can feel the touch of her father's hand on her shoulder.

*   *   *

In America, she'd been taken one day to a Burger King by Christine, who didn't connect the burgers on offer to the cows that Sita could not consume. Sita nibbled at onion rings and stared as the couple seated at the neighboring table fought with each other. They had no problem expressing themselves. They were not impeded by helplessness, caught between divergent controlling impulses that urged them to act in one way and simultaneously forced them to hold back.

They shouted freely, back and forth. They called each other names. Their words jumped on top of each other, muscled each other to the ground.

You whore, he said. You'll do anything for money. You fucking whore.

You started it, asshole, she said. Fuck you.

Eventually, the woman burst into tears and ran into the bathroom. While she was away, the man picked up her coffee cup and spat into it, stirring his rage deep, so she could swallow it down when she returned. Sita tried to control her nausea and heard Christine say: "I hope you won't mind me saying this, but in America, it's considered bad manners to stare."

Her father flies past her, pulling her mother's life behind him. The socialite raises a bottle to her lips and drinks.

Sita's hands tighten around the balcony rail. The conflict and loss within her suddenly begin to change form.

She says out loud, words mixing with angry flecks of saliva: You whores, she says. You fucking whores. You'll do anything for money.

And she can feel herself stepping back, away from the balcony.

★ ★ ★

She will now return to the office.

She will go to her computer, and use her mouse to select the folder marked SigmaSoft. All her research, all her hard work. And then she will carefully drag that folder and all its contents straight to the Recycle Bin. Trash. Gone. Deleted. There you go, everybody. And then she will spit on them and laugh and make sure her tears stay well concealed.

She walks slowly to the lift and presses the button. When the door opens, the lift-boy smiles and says, Had your coffee, madam?

Yes, Sita says. I did.

BIRDIE
NUM-NUM

It is two days after her twenty-seventh birthday, and Tara has returned home, to her parents' apartment in Bangalore. She spends the first morning in her old bedroom, setting up her computer and removing the posters that exist layer upon layer as an archeological debris of her popular interests (Jim Morrison over ABBA over Mickey Mouse in strange febrile promiscuity), and replacing her Betty and Veronica comic books with Rushdie, Theroux, and crime fiction.

Her movements are reflected in the mirror, which is edged with old photographs of Tara and her school friends playing dress-up, gawky giggles spilling from mouths painted bright red, in frozen contrast to the image in the mirror, clad in jeans and T-shirt and serious intent.

The tape player is another relic of her teenage years; the music scratchily echoing pubescent dreams of wanting to be part of a star-spangled banner of swedish pop tarts. *Can you hear the drums, Fernando? I remember long ago another starry night like this . . .*

Mrs. Srinivasan sits on the edge of the bed, watching Tara unpack and set up and rearrange. Her hand absently strokes the candlewick counterpane that covers the bed. It is a gently faded pink in color, bought ten years earlier to match the silk curtains that hang at the windows. She is struggling with the awareness that, after all these years, much about her daughter is strange to her. All the strangeness that comes with growing up and away. Naturally, she doesn't say so, but it is odd to think of having Tara back on a full-time, albeit short-term basis. Tara has visited her parents often, during college vacation, but every visit has been a compulsive return to childhood, a willful wallowing in old memories and behaviors. Now, however, Tara is back on work. And, already, Mrs. Srinivasan can see her looking around her room with fresh eyes, trying to make it grow up in a hurry.

Tara has vanished underneath her desk.

"Surely Appa can send someone from his office to help you with that," says Mrs. Srinivasan, in some surprise.

Tara plugs in the last cable and presses a switch. The computer monitor blooms into life.

"All done," she says. She smiles at her mother and reaches for the stack of her favorite MOMA prints that she has brought to keep her company for the next few months. Tara has been absorbed in a postgraduate existence in America; her PhD coursework is finally complete, having meandered tediously through classrooms, in front of computers, in libraries, and in hopeful professorial conferences. Now it is just the thesis that remains, and she is in India to research Indian labor policy for her thesis proposal.

"I will get you some tape for those posters," says her mother.

Tara holds aloft a spool of Scotch tape, but her mother has already left the room.

Mrs. Srinivasan eventually returns, with tape, a cup of hot coffee for Tara, and two brightly colored envelopes.

"You have returned," she says, "just in time to attend these."

Tara sips her coffee and watches her mother open the first envelope, patterned ominously in red and gold.

"The Shetty wedding," her mother says. "Their daughter is getting married. They spent a huge amount of money on her beauty treatments, you know. Nose operation, skin-lightening, weight loss. She is still ugly like a monkey, but her mother talks as if she is a beauty queen. You are much better looking, without a doubt. They say the boy is settled in a good banking job in Singapore, but I heard from somebody else that he just got fired. We are called to all the functions."

"Who," says Tara, "are the Shettys?"

"The Shettys! You know the Shettys. Or perhaps," says her mother, sorting through the cards, "not. There is a *sangeet* evening, the *mehndi*, the wedding itself, and the reception. There is also sure to be a young people's party. I will call and see that you are invited. You will like them," she says. "The daughter is quite charming."

"Oh," says Tara. "Thanks, Amma. But I don't think . . . I mean, I won't have time for parties and things."

"You must go. How will you meet people otherwise?"

"I will be busy working, Amma. I'm not really here to meet people."

"If you are here and do not attend, it will not look nice. We will talk about it later. This other invite, I know you will be pleased about." Tara instantly grows more wary as her mother picks up the cream-colored envelope decorated with a large Om symbol. "This is for your Vasu Athimber's birthday, his *Shashtiab-dapoorthi*."

"Heavens, is he just turning sixty? I thought he was much older."

"That is because he suffers from prostate trouble, poor man. Anyway, you can meet and catch up with your cousins. I don't think you are keeping in close touch with them."

Vasu Athimber is married to her father's second cousin. Tara glances at her mother, who meets her gaze and defies her to re-fuse this invitation also.

Some serious negotiating is in the offing. But perhaps not today.

Mrs. Srinivasan's hand hovers over the stove, poised to bestow a spicy benediction into the oil heating in the *kalchatti*, the rounded black stone vessel reposing like a museum piece on top of the fancy gas range with the four burners, the built-in hot plate, the grill, and the electric oven. Mrs. Srinivasan is a purist; she received the kalchatti from her mother when she set up her first kitchen after her marriage, and she has used it to make *vathal kuzhambu* for thirty years. Teflon and Pyrex dishes may abound in her kitchen, but in some matters, she believes, tradi-tional ways are best.

She likes to think that the kitchen has always captured the essence of their family life. The perimeter of pantry, storeroom, and countertops act like a newspaper headline—one glance and you know the news of the day: houseguests, dinner party, schooltime or holidays, major illnesses, festivals. Today it wears all the signs of Tara's homecoming dinner. Subbu, the cook, has prepared the fiery, watery *rasam,* the cabbage-and-peas *poriyal,* and the potato roast, and now stands to one side, proudly wearing the Casio watch that Tara has bought for him. He has cooked for them since Mrs. Srinivasan's marriage, except for the times, like today, when she likes to make the "special dish."

Tara walks in, to the sputter and pop of mustard seeds dancing with the other spices in the stone kalchatti.

"Finished unpacking?" Mrs. Srinivasan asks.

She can feel her daughter standing at her right elbow, just where it is most obstructive to her movements. Sometimes Tara's inexperience in the kitchen really shows. Mrs. Srinivasan quickly adds the washed curry leaves to the hot oil and spices, and is engulfed by a volcanic eruption of steam that nudges her daughter away.

Tara wanders around the kitchen, investigating the contents of the stainless steel *kadais* that lie decorously covered on the granite kitchen counter, awaiting their turn to be heated and served for lunch. It is the same menu that greets her every time she comes home; the utterly priceless constituents of all the homesick meals she has ever eaten in her cold country dreams. "Yeah," she says. "Just some reference books and papers left. I'll do that after lunch. Is that a new fridge, Amma?"

Mrs. Srinivasan smiles; she didn't think Tara would notice. She picks up the bowl of tamarind soaking in water and works the flesh with her fingers, loosening the pulp from the fiber and mixing it well with the water. Then, using her loosely cupped fingers as a strainer, she filters the brew directly into the kalchatti, relishing the hiss that rises as it strikes the oil, carrying the sharp bite of tamarind straight to the nose.

"You know, I really should learn to cook this stuff." Tara is back at her elbow, watching the process with great interest. "Maybe I'll learn this trip."

Mrs. Srinivasan should be thrilled to hear this, but, in fact, she has much larger plans for her daughter during this visit than just learning to cook. Or completing that old PhD, for that matter.

Mrs. Srinivasan likes to rest after lunch with a novel, but today her mind is restless with plans. Her novel lies unread, her eyes wander over the pile of gifts that Tara has brought home to her parents and that are heaped on the bed. A Rosenthal decorative plate; single malt whisky and sports shirts for her father; cosmetics and perfume for her mother. A bottle of dry Amontillado sherry, which Mrs. Srinivasan inspects dubiously. She is used to her Bristol Cream, which combines the merit of being a sherry with all the sweetness she requires in her evening drink. Tara has tried to nudge her out of the habit. ("You may as well drink Pepsi and get it over with.") Mrs. Srinivasan suspects that this new bottle is another of her daughter's attempts to upgrade her.

The best way, she finally decides, is to plan a cocktail party in the house.

That is something Tara cannot avoid, cannot manufacture some silly excuse to escape. Mrs. Srinivasan has waited patiently for years, for a lifetime of dealing with her daughter has given her patience to rival geological time. But now she has made up her mind: on this visit, Tara will be presented properly to all her friends. Not just casually, on a home-for-the-holidays, oh-hello-aunty basis, but properly, as someone who might one day be part of their own families. She is all too aware of the calendar. In three short years Tara will be thirty. And by that time, Mrs. Srinivasan fully intends to hold a grandchild in her arms.

"And how is Madam, madam?"

"My mother's fine, thank you. In fact, there she is." Tara turns her attention from the head steward of the Club and sips her gin-and-tonic as she waits for her mother to join her. Around her, wood-paneled walls soar up to the high ceiling, displaying a collection of stiff-necked animal heads; gloomy, glassy-eyed, decapitated and stuffed decades earlier by Englishmen crazed by the noonday sun, captured also on the Club wall in photographs, posing with catch and game and natives, and staring in turn with glassy-eyed gloom at the same natives disporting themselves in their club, in their chairs, affecting the mannerisms that they had once patented.

Mrs. Srinivasan seats herself opposite Tara, placing an over-stuffed shopping bag on the floor and arranging her saree dexterously about her knees. "So tiring! The Club stores are so crowded," she says. "Did you meet your friend Rohini? She's married, isn't she? Yes, I thought so, so nice. Are you ready to go? No, no, finish your drink."

She waves to a friend across the room. "Poor woman!" she says. Tara is probably not paying attention, but Mrs. Srinivasan's mouth runs on from old habit. "Her daughter, getting divorced, no children. And her son, they say, is having a *boy*friend. Such shame! In my day, such things were not even spoken of."

To her surprise, Tara looks at her quite seriously. "All of which is happening for a reason, you know."

"What reason?"

"Well, see," says Tara. "Look at the changes that have taken place over the past hundred years."

Her mother, who is fifty-one, tries unsuccessfully to do so.

"The species," says Tara, "is not threatened anymore. We have a sufficiently large population to ensure survival."

"What species?"

"Human beings, Amma. And furthermore, look at the changes in technology. That explains a lot."

"What technology?"

"Reproductive technology. To create a viable baby, the sperm doesn't have to meet the egg in the womb anymore. They can meet in a petri dish."

Mrs. Srinivasan glances at the approaching waiter, to see if he has overheard this embarrassingly explicit conversation. She shakes her head at Tara. Later, we can talk about this later, she wants to say, but Tara is already continuing:

"In fact, they don't even have to meet. Babies can be cloned."

"What does all this rubbish have to do with that poor woman's son and daughter?"

"I'm telling you. Because of these changes, women can now delay or cancel their breeding without threatening the species. And that's what you're seeing nowadays. And furthermore, for the same reason, if you're inclined to sexual experimentation or same-sex relationships, you can go right ahead. The human sexual relationship," says Tara, "has been forever freed from the Need to Breed. What are you doing all this shopping for?"

Mrs. Srinivasan is shocked. "For the party. Tomorrow evening. What else?"

"Oh, gosh, Amma. What a waste of energy. Don't fritter away your time on this. I brought a movie from the video store that I want you to see when we get home. It's an absolute classic."

"Is it?" Mrs. Srinivasan says, vaguely, her mind once again on the menu for tomorrow evening. She is always careful to maintain a nice blend of Indian and international foods for her parties. This time they will start with batter-fried baby corn with a peanut satay dip, and hummus, served with carrot wedges and that expensive broccoli that she acquired after a four-day stakeout at the Club's cold storage supplier. Mushroom vol-au-vents and minced mutton kebabs. Grilled chicken and pesto canapés. Delightfully crisp cocktail samosas with a tangy chutney. Those shrimp and bacon things that people seem to enjoy so much. What on earth does Tara call them? Angels on horseback, yes. The food will be a hit, Mrs. Srinivasan knows. It always is. She declines a drink, impatient to get home and check if the cook is doing everything on schedule.

"Are you going to wear that new *salwar-khameez* suit that I bought you?" she asks.

"What, right now?" Tara asks, astonished.

"No. Tomorrow. For the party," Mrs. Srinivasan says. "Are you going to wear that? What are you going to wear?" This is the third time she has asked the question over the past few days, but she has never received a satisfactory answer.

"Dear god," Tara says. "Amma, why don't you just think about what *you* are going to wear."

"Oh, I haven't decided," says Mrs. Srinivasan, though she has. It will be fun to discuss her options with Tara, and to look at the sarees together. . . . Perhaps Tara will decide to wear a saree also. A vision of her daughter elegantly dressed appears tantalizingly in her mind.

Tara catches the pleased smile on her mother's face and smiles back. She places her empty glass on a side table and inclines her head towards the exit. "Coming to see this movie or not?"

Mrs. Srinivasan hesitates. There is a lot to be done around the house, but it can wait awhile. "All right," she says. "What is this movie?"

"One of my favorites. It's witty, it's brilliant. A real classic."

"*Roman Holiday*?" Mrs. Srinivasan asks hopefully. She is very fond of Audrey Hepburn.

Tara picks up her mother's shopping bag; the headwaiter ducks his head ingratiatingly as the two women leave the clubhouse.

The music blares, the titles roll.

Tara glances at her mother, wondering what she will think of it. Mrs. Srinivasan looks startled, her attention riveted to the television screen. Tara settles back, mouthing the dialogue along with the actors in the movie. It has been a while since she has last seen it, but she stills knows chunks of the film by heart. "*Do you know what they call a Quarter Pounder with Cheese in Paris? . . . a Royale with Cheese . . .*"

* * *

Later, Mrs. Srinivasan's lips are still pursed. She tries to look enthusiastic. "It was . . . interesting. Quite interesting. Except," she cannot help saying, "for that dreadful language."

"Ungrammatical, you mean?"

"Tchi! It was full of Bad language! Why do they use it?"

"Fuck knows," Tara says, but only to herself.

"It's so unnecessary!"

"Amma, it's a movie about American gangsters. You can't expect the Queen's English."

"No, but still . . ."

Tara starts to laugh. "Can you imagine . . ." She assumes an exaggerated English accent: " 'I say, Higgins, old chap, take a pop at that ruddy blighter.' . . . 'After you, Pickering, old fellow. I insist.' . . . 'I desired the waiter in Paris to bring me a minced beef sandwich. Except those French chappies call it a Le Beeg Mac.' . . . 'Not really. How droll.' . . ."

"Now, *that* is what I call a good movie," says her mother. "*My Fair Lady*. Good music, romantic, witty, lovely costumes . . . Which reminds me," she says, "what are you going to wear for the party?"

Tara asks, foolishly, ignorantly: Why does it matter so much what I wear?

"One must be well dressed for such occasions," Mrs. Srinivasan says, inadequately, she feels.

I will be, says Tara. Well dressed. I have been, she says, for years.

"Good! So, what are your choices? Did you bring anything nice from America? If you don't like that salwar-khameez, you can wear one of my sarees. I have one that will look lovely on you. With your long hair carefully dressed, and that saree, you will look like a goddess . . . not like that Shetty girl, poor thing. She is scrawny like a starving mouse."

As she speaks, she can see her daughter's face turn towards her in startled comprehension, but it is too late, she cannot recall the words.

Please don't tell me, Tara says, that *that's* what this party is all about.

And Mrs. Srinivasan is forced to say: "What nonsense! Why can I not throw a party for my friends when my daughter comes home? . . . Matchmaking? What nonsense! Why do you say such things? I think you forget who you are talking to. No, it is you who are fussing over such a tiny thing!"

Tara walks out, but not before her mother hears her say, implausibly: What makes you think I'm going to attend this stupid party?

The sound of the door slamming shut reverberates through the walls and right through Mrs. Srinivasan's belly. She knows that her daughter is only joking, she has to be—inconceivable to think of absenting herself from her parents' party, such disrespect—but still, Mrs. Srinivasan feels the whine of tension tighten around her spine.

The fact is, somewhere along the way Tara has drifted away from her. Now she seems to take after her father instead—freewheeling, impulsive, and self-absorbed when it comes to domestic matters. Mrs. Srinivasan instinctively rebels against this arrangement of things. Behavior that she will excuse and compensate for in her husband is intolerable in her grown-up daughter. After all, men will be men, but shouldn't daughters be a support?

And here, Mrs. Srinivasan knows herself to be the victim of a time warp. It isn't fair, being trained to do something all your life, and then, when it is too late to change, being told that it was all a mistake. By the way, a woman's place isn't in the kitchen. How silly you are, you and your kitty parties. Sometimes she doesn't even know whether things have really changed all that much, or whether Tara assumed some attitude, like today, just to shock her.

Didn't young women dream of marriage anymore?

Was her daughter not lonely?

Her hand automatically straightens the remote controls into a line. There are three of them, one each for the TV, the VCR, and the DVD player, and Mrs. Srinivasan sometimes finds it difficult to tell them apart.

Tara pours herself a snifter of cognac from her father's bar and wanders out onto the terrace garden of the sprawling penthouse apartment. Lavelle Road reposes below in a midnight hush. Behind her, the house is quiet. Her parents are asleep, the servants have long since retired. Tara stands in a blanket of darkness: a lonely lamp diffuses the shadows within the house, but doesn't penetrate to where she stands; the street below is barely lit, the streetlights in perpetual dysfunction. The dark is echoed in the heavy cloud cover above. There is no rain, but the southwest winds whip past, forcing the monsoon onwards. Tara shivers in the chill, glad of the shawl she has wrapped around herself. She sips her fiery drink, inhaling the fumes from the glass held warm in the cup of her hand.

When Tara turned eighteen, her parents gifted her with all the further education she could possibly want, along with a tacit understanding that she would be free to choose anyone she liked for a life-mate. A rare, delightful freedom, which Tara fully appreciated, until she grew older and realized that it carried, cunningly concealed within it, a set of maternal expectations embedded like land mines, with the ability to detonate through her life when she least expected it. She had been gifted with the freedom to choose—but not the freedom to delay. Or to refuse. Or to change her mind, no thanks, maybe later, I don't feel like it, don't-call-me-about-it-I'll-call-you. Especially once she turned twenty-five.

This visit had promised to be different. Tara had hoped that seeing her return home on work would give her mother a different perspective, one that was more closely allied with Tara's view of herself. Where her mother focused happily, as she used to, on the things that Tara *had* achieved, instead of chasing after her with the terrible question that dogged her through all her recent visits, from the moment she stepped off the just-landed plane: Have you found Anyone Special yet?

An autorickshaw rumbles by, the noise echoing in the quiet of the street.

The shadows of the prostitutes sidle along the pavement, merging every now and then with cars that slow down, stop, and then continue on their way. The police are busy: their whistles sound in intermittent haunting monotones, informing the sleeping citizens that they could rest in peace, and also encouraging the prostitutes to have a successful night; for the policemen, who believe in the Nehruvian socialist ideal that the public sector should support private industry, would be around for their percentage later.

Her friend Rohini had once asked her whether her mother knew about Derek. And all Tara could think was, Oh yes, that would make for a lovely conversation. "Mother, you know how you keep asking if I've found someone? Well, I did, and then he found someone else and didn't tell me about it, so to answer your question, technically no, I haven't." Though, in the misery of the months that followed, Tara had more than once reached for the phone, her fingers dialing the number home. And each time, she had put the phone down, never quite sure if the comfort she needed was the comfort her mother could provide.

And, now, there was this foolish, foolish party.

Did her mother not see how demeaning it was?

From her perch four floors above street level, she has a good view of the city skyline. It has remained unchanged her entire life, and, on every visit, she has gone through the ritual of identifying all the nighttime sights of home: the lone red light atop the Unity Building glowing in the distance as a warning to low-flying (extremely low-flying, practically landed type of low-flying) aircraft; the dark host of trees silhouetted against the orange haze of the sodium vapor lamps that light Mahatma Gandhi Road. And on the other side, the dense mass of Cubbon Park in the distance; and beyond, the peculiar monolithic Life Insurance Corporation building, shaped like a submarine, and vainglorious Vidhana

Soudha, seat of governmental inefficiencies, illumined with all the light that is kept in such short supply to the rest of the city.

Mrs. Srinivasan leans against the bar and looks around with a feeling of quiet satisfaction. The penthouse looks beautiful in the fading dusk light. The sloping wooden roof gleams with mansion polish. The marble floor has been scrubbed twice with soap and water. She turns the main chandelier on, and gently tones down the brightness of the beam to a gentle glow that will deepen with the dusk, until the wooden roof above gleams red. The lights play off the Baccarat dolphins, and over the dark wood of the piano and the mahogany Masai carvings that she bought three years ago while on safari in Kenya.

The piano is an old English baby grand that Mrs. Srinivasan still practices on religiously every day. A long, long time ago, Mrs. Srinivasan started Tara on piano lessons, her mind filled with young-mother dreams of playing duets with her daughter to an admiring audience of her friends. Dreams that, like so many others, have fallen blithely away. Tara refused to buckle down to the rigors of classical music, preferring to bang out the occasional show tune when she was in the mood.

Mrs. Srinivasan walks about, mentally reviewing her check-list. Crisp linen doilies, embroidered by Catholic nuns and bought at the little SSV shop off Church Street, lie scattered about. Wax candles have been placed in all the bizarre and varied candlesticks that are her passion. Of course they have an inverter for the frequent power cuts that besiege the city at the most inconvenient of times, but candlelight really does create a lovely ambiance. Matchboxes that she has hoarded over the years are layered carefully in a ceramic bowl: Taj and Oberoi hotel match-boxes at the bottom, then matches from the '21' Club in New York and Tokyo's Imperial Hotel, and finally, right on top, her favorite: POST-PRANDIAL SLINGS AT THE LONG BAR from the Raffles Hotel in Singapore.

During the party, Lily, who is the maid Elsa's daughter, will serve the snacks, while Elsa herself will wash dishes and help Subbu in the kitchen. A boy from her husband's office will serve at the bar.

Downstairs in the kitchen, the big Wedgwood plates that will hold the snacks are waiting on silver trays that Lily will carry as she has been taught—offering the guests a snack and a napkin from the dainty silver holder that rests alongside. The bar is ready: the crystal glasses have been meticulously washed, air-dried, and polished with a soft cloth and now glisten quietly on the ornate counter built from Karaikudi temple carvings. The bootlegger has been by, leaving expensive foreign whiskies and brandies in his wake for the menfolk. Wine, sherry, and soft drinks for the ladies. The after-dinner cognac and liqueurs are, strictly speaking, not necessary for a cocktail party, but people do ask for the strangest things sometimes.

Mrs. Srinivasan peeps into the powder room to ensure that the embroidered hand towels and scented soaps have been laid out ready to use, and then wanders out onto the verandah. The white-painted rattan furniture is arranged in premeditated conversation clusters around the terrace garden.

Mrs. Srinivasan loves her garden. Loves the way the sloping tiled roof and the climbing rose trellises that fall carelessly over the verandah give the house the appearance of the estate homes in which she spent the early years of her marriage, when Mr.

Srinivasan joined the Madras-Malay Trading Company as a young management trainee and was posted to the company's coffee estates all around the Nilgiri hills. The terrace garden is at tree level, and the astonishing Bangalore greenery that surrounds it and spreads in every direction almost gives one the impression of being far away in the green hills rather than in a penthouse in the middle of town.

Standing on the lawn, one can look through the long windows into the glowing drawing room. The potted flowers outside are echoed in the lavish flower arrangements within. The vases spill over in a riot of birds-of-paradise, purple gladioli, and orange carnations. Delicate orchids float in crystal bowls on the low coffee table.

She had once enrolled a prepubescent Tara in an ikebana flower-arranging course, organized by her friends on the Club Ladies Subcommittee. It would be so nice, now, if she could point to all the flower vases and say to her friends, see, that is what my daughter has done, as proof of Tara's skill in the domestic arts. But that is another idle fantasy. As with so many other things, Tara had fought her way out of doing the flowers a long time ago.

And Mrs. Srinivasan's mind cannot help asking: all said and done, what is wrong with being skilled in maintaining a good home? Career or not, women need to know this—it is an essential female something, to do with being mothers and wives, and nurturing families and societies. None of which, try though Tara might, can one negate. After all, if you look at it scientifically, the whole biological purpose of being female is to bear children. No children equals no femaleness. And without femaleness, where would her daughter's beloved feminists be?

Mrs. Srinivasan searches in her own past: had she ever clashed so with her own mother? Certainly they had argued. But, fundamentally, they had both understood the importance of women's work, disagreeing only on the best way to get it done. The rights and wrongs, for instance, of Mrs. Srinivasan supporting her husband's decision to depart from a traditional Iyer Brahmin lifestyle, and to anglicize their life in accordance with the culture of his firm. Or the wisdom of sending one's only child to America for further studies instead of, as the old lady suggested, getting her married at home.

Yes, Tara was her only child, and so Mrs. Srinivasan had sat with her through all her exams, providing endless cups of midnight coffee and moral support while Tara applied to American universities. Her mother had passed away before Mrs. Srinivasan could share with her the sense of achievement she felt when Tara eventually decided to pursue her PhD. Her husband may have a master's degree, but her daughter, Mrs. Srinivasan would have liked to have boasted, will have a Doctorate.

But now there is no doubt about it. Tara is twenty-seven, and no matter how many PhDs she earns, it is time now for her to learn to be a good wife and mother, just as her mother and grandmother have done in their turn.

Mrs. Srinivasan turns on the garden lights and crosses over to Tara's room. She hesitates; then, with old habits, opens the door without knocking. Her daughter is seated in front of her computer, entering data from a little book whose yellowed, stained pages bespeak its origins in a government office. Tara's hair is knotted messily on top of her head, her glasses are slightly askew, and Mrs. Srinivasan is assailed, once again, by worry.

"We should be ready by seven-fifteen," she says. "The guests have been invited for seven-thirty, and some of the older people, like Mr. Rao and the general, will be exactly on time. You *will* be ready, won't you?"

Tara puts down the book and turns to face her mother.

For twenty-four hours she has rehearsed the excuse that will free her from this party.

Around them, the house darkens with the night.

The bathroom mirror captures a Tara of rare elegance.

She is wearing a well-tailored jacket and pant ensemble, with a silk blouse that echoes the cappuccino color of her skin. She looks remarkably chic. She looks uneasy and awkward.

She looks furious with herself for failing, at the end, to say no to her mother.

Her long curly hair has been combed away from her face, which is newly revealed by the absence of glasses. Her contact lenses make her blink. Perhaps it is time to get them replaced.

"Birdie *num*-num," she says to her reflection, trying to catch Peter Sellers' movie imitation of an absurd little Indian gentleman at a Hollywood party Bir Die—she feels her lips meet and part, her tongue curve backwards and slap against the back of her teeth, the final horizontal stretch of her lips. Num Num. "Birdie num-num."

The party outside is in full force, the chatter penetrating her little hideaway.

Birdie num-num.

The social fossils who have infested the house can look at her with only one thought in their smelly old minds.

The men, balding, paunchy, and old-spiced, leer at her and ask: So, when's a pretty girl like you going to get married?

The women, besilked and hair-sprayed, shake their heads at her: Aren't you getting a little too old to not be settled?

I *am* "settled," thinks Tara. Unsettling to you, perhaps, but perfectly settled, thank-you-very-much.

She suggested to her father that she hang around for a while, meet everybody, then quietly exit to join her friends at the Blue Cigar Pub. Good idea, is what he should have said, sympathetically winking at her and shaking his head towards her mother.

Nonsense, Tara, was what he said. These are your guests as well. They have come to see you. You must stay and look after them. Go and help your mother.

Birdie num-num.

Back into the fray.

Her mother is everywhere, comporting herself with her usual elegance in an earth-toned saree that is as quiet as it is delicate, with solitaire diamonds twinkling discreetly from ears and finger. She is in terrifyingly full-blown form, laughing, hostessing, charming, feeding. Tara tries to keep away from her, but her mother's voice follows her around. She is talking with a resplendent blue saree that is draped around a blouse a tad too small for the body it contains.

"Yes," she says. "We have received so many offers for Tara.

But you know what girls are like nowadays. So independent. Must make up their own minds about everything." A small laugh. "Have a samosa?"

"Thank you," and stuffing another samosa into that too-tight blouse. "No, thankfully, I have not faced that problem. My daughter, who is now expecting her second child, by the way, is only too happy to listen to me. She always says that my choice is best. She is not like Tara."

"No, indeed. She is not like Tara. Few youngsters, I think, could do as well as Tara has in her PhD. Her professors in America are *very* impressed with her, you know."

Touché.

And later, elsewhere in the room:

"Tara is *so* skilled, you know . . ."

And:

". . . so many gifts for us from America . . . those Rosenthal plates . . . Even if we say no, she brings us things. . . . Yes, so lucky . . ."

And:

". . . so keen to learn the traditional recipes . . ."

Oh, mother. Must you?

Tara's fury propels her to the bar. A shot of Laphroaig in a glass and it's back to the bathroom. Her reflection stares placidly back at her, unmoved by her temper. Num-num. She sips her drink, her tongue traveling through the flavors in her glass. Ultimately, she thinks, the great argument between single malt and blended is a mood thing. A good blended whisky is a comfort drink, crooning softly to you as it nurses you in its arms. A fine single malt is a seducer: muscle-bound, sexy, and fiery-eyed, urging you to up and at 'em.

The whisky is pushing her to misbehave. *I think I will go outside and ask them* why *I need to get married, since I already have a* perfectly *active sex life. Now, that would give them something to talk about for the next ten parties.*

Now, now. Behave, birdie. Num-num to you.

Tara once again exits the bathroom.

First, a word with her mother.

"Amma, will you please stop *marketing* me? And please don't discuss my nonexistent wedding plans with everybody. It really is no one else's business."

"Don't be silly, Tara. These are our good friends. Of course I will tell them how proud I am of my child."

"I tell you, I have no intention of marrying one of their idiotic sons!"

"What nonsense you talk. You're arguing about nothing." Mother and daughter stare each other down. "Go see if your father wants any help."

Dismissed like a bloody fourteen-year-old, thinks Tara. But she goes.

And spends the rest of the party trying to convince Lily not to sample the snacks that she is serving, and ensuring that the office boy doesn't get *too* drunk behind the bar.

At the end of the party, the old general pats her cheek and says that she is a fine hostess, just like her mother.

Her parents beam with pleasure.

The next day Tara oversleeps and emerges with a mild whisky hangover and a strong sense of ill-usage. Her father is settled on the living room sofa, surrounded by newspapers and the televised blare of PGA golf, happily snacking on party leftovers. Her mother has the happy, tired air of someone who has been organizing, putting away, getting things back to normal after a very successful party.

"So many people called," she says. "Such a lovely evening, they said . . . wonderful snacks . . ."

Tara refuses to participate in this happy postmortem. She is sulking and aloof.

Her mother prattles on. Her father is mellowed, relaxed, with the happy unwariness of a man who, having locked away the last whisky bottle the previous night and toted up, in awed tones, the amount of alcohol consumed at the party, knows that nothing further is expected of him.

Tara is brooding, formal, stiff in her responses. She waits for her mother to slowly approach the topic at hand, to push the conversation into discussions of the people who attended, their families, and the wondrous eligibility of their sons. She waits patiently, for a lifetime of dealing with her mother has given her the patience to rival geological time. She waits to deliver the scathing rebuff that will forever stop her mother from interfering in her life.

But Mrs. Srinivasan veers away from the subject completely.

She has vanished into her bedroom, and now reappears.

"Tara," she says. "I need assistance in getting some boxes down. Could you help me, please?"

All of Tara's latent irritation swells up, but before she can speak, her eyes fall on her mother's face, which is lined with fatigue and suddenly seems pulled down by the weight of her years.

"Okay," she says, and walks into her mother's bedroom.

Mrs. Srinivasan directs her daughter as she climbs a stool and pulls down the boxes and old bags that are needed for storage. Then, and only then, does she artfully revert to her real reason for calling Tara into her bedroom.

"You know, I was sorting through these old sarees of mine the other day . . ." She carelessly indicates the pile lying on the bed.

Tara's attention is caught by the pretty colors of the silks. "Oh, I remember these. They're lovely, Amma. Why don't you wear them anymore?"

Mrs. Srinivasan wants to say: I was saving them for you. Do you like them? Would you like to wear them? I hope you do. How lovely it would be to see you enjoying something that belonged to me.

Instead she says: "One has to be young to wear colors and designs like that. They don't look good on someone who's crossed fifty."

Tara opens the sarees; her hands play across the fine old silk. Her mother watches her growing absorption with a deep, eager pleasure and then pulls out a package from the recesses of her cupboard.

"Oh, what's this?"

The sun shines through the window and highlights the deep red of the saree, that *arakku,* the glorious color not quite blood, not quite claret, and gleams off the heavy, intricately patterned gold-work of the *zari.*

"This is my wedding saree." Mrs. Srinivasan inexplicably feels a strange diffidence in front of her daughter. She sits down next to her and strokes the old saree with tentative, gentle hands. "Paati had to go to Kanjeevaram to get it specially made for me."

Tara's grandmother had led a mysterious, antediluvian life in Madras, her wrinkled softness forever clad in a traditional nine-yard saree, her forehead smeared with piousness and holy *vibhooti* ash.

Her mother's wedding saree is also nine yards long, three yards longer than a modern saree, and Tara touches it curiously.

Would you like to try it on? her mother says.

Tara pulls off her jeans, and her mother drapes the saree around her and between her legs, finally arranging the *thalaippu,* the decorative end-piece, in a tuck around her waist. Her long hair is smoothed back and twisted quickly into a knot at the nape of her neck. She walks slowly across to the full-length mirror, reluctance warring with curiosity.

Seventy years have fallen away, and Tara stares mesmerized.

She has been transformed into her grandmother.

Her Paati, young, ripe, and full of life, laughs at her from the mirror.

And behind her, her mother, her daughter, smiles back.

APPLE PIE,
ONE BY TWO

There is nothing very offensive about Murthy, even when he is high. He is usually rather quiet, but after two joints he becomes a little more effusive, and rather predictable. There are two things he likes to do, but even those he does more for his own benefit than anyone else's. The first is to appropriate the music system and play Dave Drubeck's "Take Five" twice over. As it plays, he likes to nod his head and spell out the rhythm: FOUR FIVE, One Two Three FOUR FIVE. His gaze is locked inwards in musical bliss, and everyone else lets him be.

The second thing he likes to do is to paraphrase a minor character in the Billy Bunter books he loved so much as a child.

This is, very occasionally, on a night like this. Otherwise, during the day, he displays his skills as a software engineer, joins his friends for a drink and a little conversation after work, and lives quietly with his parents. His mother refers to him affectionately as a good boy. Friends like Swamy, though equally affectionate, refer to him in terms somewhat less complimentary, and Murthy reciprocates in turn.

The cheap glass that Swamy holds in his hand is almost empty, and Murthy's face is refracted through it, stretching and wobbling in peculiar ways. It is a face that, like the sky, has accompanied Swamy everywhere, through school, engineering college, work, and life in two countries; usually mirroring his own aspirations and desires. But that, of course, is about to change; and Swamy studies Murthy's face with a faint puzzlement that refuses to go away.

They are not alone, Murthy and Swamy. Other faces shift around them, shadowed and illumined by the night and the bonfire around which they sit. The glow of the fire is offset by a lone electrical bulb that swings from the rafters of the *dhaba* that lies to one side of the clearing: a meager shed insulated from the night chill by the heat of the wood-burning stove, and by the evanescent, spicy odors that rise from the food bubbling on top—succulent roasting chicken coated with chili and lime, glistening in the heat; hot wheat rotis on the *tava* pan; spicy vegetable *subzis;* lentils. The proprietor-and-cook stands over the stove, bare-chested, a dirty dhoti wrapped sarong-style around his waist, his forehead marked with a frown of concentration and beaded with perspiration. It is his customers who wait outside by the bonfire, stretched out on the charpoys that are scattered around the clearing, self-consciously absorbing themselves in the cool beauty of the night. The charpoys themselves, beds of rope woven around a light wooden frame, seem as old as the earth they rest on, and creak and rock with every movement.

* ★ *

This was supposed to be a much smaller group of people, but it hadn't quite worked out that way. The party they had attended earlier in the evening had been a mistake. Swamy had felt restless; this was not how he wanted to spend his last evening in Bangalore. It was Murthy who suggested an alternative: to leave the party, drive out of the city, find a dhaba on the highway and dine alfresco. A meal, in short, that would take them back to their undergraduate days, when dhabas had been steady sources of cheap nourishment; dhaba proprietors usually, with great financial empathy, allowed them to share food and conserve money by dividing the item ordered into separate servings as per the request: one-by-two (single dish, between two people) or two-by-three or, on really impecunious days, one-by-three. Coffee one-by-two, and Murthy and Swamy could sit there for the rest of the day, clinging to their half-filled cups.

Swamy was delighted with the idea; but just as they were about to leave the party with a couple of close friends, someone else got wind of where they were going, and next thing you know, it had turned into a circus. Three cars, full of people, roaring down the highway, and here they all were.

"You big-mouthed bastard," Swamy accused Murthy, a little unfairly. Murthy is still one of the quietest individuals he knows.

This particular dhaba is a lucky find; relatively clean, relatively free of the truckers who are the main clientele of such places. The dhaba owner seems used to feeding wandering tribes of urbanites who happen by with their fancy cars and unreal economics; without comment, he has lighted the coal *sigri* that holds the fire, pulled up charpoys, and offered them bottles of cold Kingfisher beer to drink. And this is enough, for the moment, to keep Swamy content; to allow him to stretch out, empty his mind of all the decisions that have dogged him for months, and ponder the residual surprise that still rises within him when he looks at Murthy.

At least, so it would be, if it weren't for the conversation people keep forcing on him—he is under cheerful verbal attack from two individuals he met at the party earlier in the evening, and who do not seem to recognize that they are not wanted. They both appear to want to convince him that he is doing the right thing.

"I think it's damn good, *yaar*, damn good," says Rahul.

"Oh, yeah," says Karl. "I wish I were in your shoes."

"The last time," says Rahul, "in Las Vegas, I tell you, I couldn't decide whether to keep my eyes on the tables or on those chicks. Leaning over to serve drinks, their tits almost falling out. Great country!"

"Tell me about it!"

Swamy grunts and leans back.

"And then New York. What nightclubs, just too cool. And the shopping is something else. Everything so cheap. Half the price of London." Rahul, Swamy is learning, suffers from a surfeit of inherited money and a depressing lack of imagination. He asks Swamy, "Where do you do your shopping?"

"I don't shop."

"Ah, good joke!" says Rahul, but he is looking discouraged. Swamy is one of the new fairy tales, someone who has founded and sold a software company that everyone talks about and venture capitalists see in their favorite visions. Swamy should be shopping.

"Ask Murthy," says Swamy, relenting. "When we first shared

an apartment, in America, he kept shopping. It was an obsession with him."

Across the fire, he can see Murthy laughing in response.

The first of two apartments that Murthy and Swamy shared was a tiny place; just off-campus and furnished very simply, with a mattress on the floor of each bedroom in lieu of a bed, and another mattress in the tiny living room in lieu of a sofa. That was when they were graduate students, newly arrived from India, at the University of Pennsylvania. In the kitchen, they diligently acquired a pot for the rice, a pot for the dal lentils, a pan for the vegetables, a fridge that didn't work, and a book full of handwritten recipes contributed to by their worried mothers in every letter from home. When Swamy announced casually that he had bought a television, he spent a moment savoring the distress on Murthy's face at such unwarranted profligacy, before adding, "Black-and-white for twenty-eight dollars." They had celebrated this acquisition with cheap beer and an evening spent injudiciously coaxing the antenna to capture a new show called *Seinfeld*.

It had come as a shock, at first, to discover exactly how poor they were.

Their college scholarships covered their tuition, and little else. Like their American colleagues, they worked at other jobs for their living expenses. Unlike the Americans, however, their student visas prevented them from working at reasonable rates off-campus, so they provided cheap intellectual grunt labor for anyone who asked. They taught undergraduates, did research for professors, worked in computer labs. And, again unlike the Americans, they could not rely on student loans, credit cards, or

easy access to their parents' homes and the acquisitions of a lifetime for material comfort. No cold-weather clothes, no car, no
microwave, no popcorn maker. No Christmas presents of a golf
set, or a tennis racquet, or a nice winter coat that happened to be
on sale at Neiman Marcus.

They didn't think of asking their parents in India for financial
support; neither of them was so irresponsible. Murthy's father
was an accountant; Swamy's a lawyer. Their respective incomes
allowed them to maintain their families in decent homes, provide a good education for their children, a maid to help their
wives with the housework, and annual holidays in the hill sta-
tions of Ooty or Kodaikanal. In India, the money stretched that
far. Converted into dollars, it simply vanished, reduced to a sum
insufficient to buy a decent car even. The economy-class plane
ticket to America had cost their parents two months' income,
and that was all anyone could expect. In return for that gift, their
sons were expected to take no risks, work twice as hard as the
Americans, and eventually land good jobs, get married, and produce, lickety-split, so many grandchildren and raise them with
good old-fashioned Indian values.

Luckily, Swamy and Murthy were not alone. Most of the
Indians who came to study in America acted as they did, teeter-
ing between poverty on the one hand and grand future prospects
on the other. There was a comfort in this, in meeting in each
other's rooms to eat dal and rice and feel a little less homesick, to
figure out what jobs were being offered by what companies and
how best to tackle the interviews.

Occasionally they would run into that other breed of Indian
abroad. "Usually," said Murthy, paraphrasing another favorite
author, "the kind of thing one sees in bad dreams, or when one is

out without one's gun." A breed that, like Rahul, was the product of inherited money; that meticulously failed all the exams
and bought a Mercedes-Benz as a reward; and that subsequently
vanished back to the homeland to don suit, glasses, and foreign
credentials, before giving interviews that nobody believed on
the need to introduce professional managers into family-run
businesses.

It was Murthy, even then, who kept a strict control over their
finances. He would plan and budget, wandering around the
supermarkets with coupons in one hand and a calculator in
the other, saying no to the handmade pasta, and yes to the
big cheap tub of rice. "There's a sale on," he'd say, meaning not
Bloomingdale's or even Kmart, but the secondhand sale by some
other graduate student who'd gotten a job somewhere and was
selling everything before moving uptown, upscale. A sale, and
Murthy and Swamy would rush across to buy (on a predeter-
mined budget) perhaps a cooking pot, or a winter jacket that
with a little effort could have the stains removed.

All of which is presumably not the kind of shopping Rahul
has in mind.

"Is there anything to smoke?" asks Ashwini. Swamy hunts for his
cigarettes, while Rahul pulls out his cigars.

"Ah, the dog turds," says Swamy.

"Cohiba Esplendidos," says Rahul. "Try them. They're very
good."

Ashwini eagerly reaches for one. She is technically Murthy's
girlfriend, and patently hopes to be something more. She has
read about fashionable women who smoke cigars, and she is

keen to emulate them. Rahul courteously trims the end of a cigar for her, and then shows her how to light it by holding it not in, but over, the flame, and the importance of puffing without inhaling. Ashwini is pleased, and punctuates everything she says with waves of the thick stub between her fingers.

Murthy, on the other hand, looks disappointed. "Shit," he says. "Nothing apart from tobacco?"

"I may have something," says Swamy. "In the car." He and Murthy exchange glances, each willing the other to shake the laziness from his feet, get up, and go to the car.

"I'll go," says Ashwini.

She returns with a small tin box, which Murthy appropriates and reverently opens. "Kerala Gold," he says, sniffing deeply. "The best fucking grass south of Manali."

He proceeds to roll two joints with the concentration that he brings to all important tasks, before lighting one, inhaling, and passing it on.

As young schoolboys, they had gone through a phase of reading Billy Bunter, enjoying the antics of the English school boys, and puzzled by the little Indian prince's inability to speak a word of comprehensible English. Or as the English author would have His Royal Highness, Hurree Jamset Ram Singh, Nabob of Bhanipur (called "Inky" by his associates), say: the incomprehensiblefulness of the spoken English in its very mystification is terrific.

The other thing Murthy likes to do when he is high is to paraphrase the little nabob; to say, every now and then:

The Thingfulness of the Thing
In its very Thingness
Is so Thing.

This is a lispy mouthful even when sober; when Murthy is high he seems rather proud of being able to say it at all.

Now Swamy waits patiently, but before Murthy can speak, Rahul is already turning his head inquisitively towards him.

"You were based in Palo Alto, right?" Rahul's persistence shows that a party invitation will soon be in the offing. Couple of those, and then Rahul will be able to tell everyone that yes, Swamy is a good, damn good, friend of his.

"After graduate school, yes," says Swamy.

Their second apartment was very different from the first, and not just because it entailed a shift to California from their previous East Coast university existence. By the time they graduated, both Murthy and Swamy were sought after by different software corporations, and they had finally signed on, with enormous bonuses, with the same one.

"What are your housing plans?" Murthy had asked, not lifting his eyes from his bank statement, which, post-bonus, exercised a strong fascination over him.

Swamy's reply had been prompt. "A house in Palo Alto," he'd said. With a lemon tree on the side and a new (no, not second-hand, never) car parked in the drive.

"That's expensive," Murthy said, mindful of the fact that Swamy, like himself, was a dutiful son, and would be sending money home to his parents.

"Yeah," said Swamy. He hesitated; now that they had a choice, he was suddenly reluctant to put Murthy on the spot. "I was actually planning on a roommate. Maybe advertise for one, or something. You?"

Oh, something similar, Murthy said. Or, bastard, maybe I'll just answer your advertisement.

They bought furniture from Ikea, with king-size beds in each room, which would prove useful when they brought girls home. They argued over the merits of Ford Escorts and Honda Accords, but finally settled on buying Toyota Corollas, one each but in different colors, taking turns parking them in the one-car garage. They shopped at good stores and ate in nice restaurants. They worked out and ate health food from different countries and made interesting friends who spoke intelligently and well and played jazz on the weekends. They were finally living the American Dream.

Or half of it, at any rate. The other half proved far more elusive.

"And the chicks," says Rahul, "in California. Really pretty. You must have seen some serious action, yaar."

"Serious," says Swamy, deadpan. "But Murthy was the real swinger." And Murthy avoids Rahul's respectful glance to raise his middle finger discreetly at Swamy.

The moonlight slowly seeps into their collective consciousness. Conversation slows down before it really begins, flaring up here and there in a languid, desultory way. Ashwini has shifted over to sit on the floor, next to Murthy, still puffing tentatively on her cigar, rounding her lips and swirling the smoke with her tongue in an effort to produce smoke rings. Across the fire, Swamy can see Murthy's hand resting gently upon her shoulder.

Their undergraduate dreams of America had focused on the great universities there, but frequently segued to something far more tantalizing; for their engineering class in India had been subdivided by subject matter (electronics, mechanical, civil, chemical)—and also by sexual experience. A very small, elite percentage actually had girlfriends, and sex with those girlfriends. Another small chunk had sex and paid for it, usually from the prostitute who lived up the road. They would queue outside her hut, and after each client she would step outside and wash her bottom out with cold water from the bucket near the door before taking in the next customer. Then there was the festering majority (to which Murthy and Swamy belonged), who were a little more fastidious and had remained appallingly virginal. America, Land of the Blonde and Home of the Brazen, pioneer of UnMarital Sex, would surely change all that. America, whose streets were lined, it was said, with vending-machine girls who lay naked, with welcoming signs painted over slots between their spread-eagled legs that said, For a Treat, Insert Here.

But that, like so many Hollywood-inspired dreams, was pure marketing hype.

Not government endorsed.

Swamy's first American girlfriend turned out to be significantly non-blonde, a Punjabi woman he met in graduate school. Indian, yes, but she'd grown up in America, and might therefore be more willing to put out. She was; and for that reason alone, Swamy unashamedly stayed with her. He didn't like her very much, but he was deeply grateful.

Not so Murthy.

A hundred attempts and near misses, and Murthy got so desperate that he had taken to driving repeatedly past the ladies who offered their professional services on a certain corner of El Camino, and who would ask him softly, "Want some poontang, honey?" He did, decidedly so, but a remnant of his earlier fastidiousness kept him from formalizing any business relationship with them.

In fact, Murthy may well be a virgin even today, though that cannot be held against him. Swamy does not know this for a fact. Up to a certain age, one advertises the momentous loss of one's virginity; beyond that, one keeps quiet and loses it as best as one can. Ashwini certainly does not appear to be concerned.

Dinner arrives halfway through their second drink, the welcome clatter of plates galvanizing them. Swamy's mouth suddenly waters, as if anticipating a future when it will be denied such flavors, in such surroundings. The dhaba owner carries out trays full of dishes, accompanied and aided by two dusty rag-encased urchins who stare at the visitors with bright, curious eyes. The food is straight from the tava, sizzling with heat and spices that set eyes watering and tongues screaming for more: chicken sixty-five, pepper mutton, kebabs. Hot rotis are placed on old steel plates weighed down further by dal and vegetables and chicken gravy. Nobody waits upon ceremony: teeth tear hungrily at the fragrant meat, while fingers scoop chopped onion and lime into eager open mouths.

"Leave something for me, bugger," says Murthy, laughing at Swamy's eagerness.

"Order another plate, you stingy bastard," Swamy says. "This one's mine."

"Fine, I'll order one more," says Murthy, "but you're paying for it."

We'll split it, says Swamy. One-by-two.

It had all started in idle conversation, late one night.

Swamy and Murthy sat at conjoined desks that competed in clutter with the other desks around, problem solving for the big software company that employed them in Palo Alto. The office lights were dimmed, except at odd locations where clots of people worked under fluorescent lighting that did not disguise the bags of fatigue under their eyes, or the late-night sour smell of too little sleep and take-out food that surrounded them. Swamy had finally produced what looked like a solution for a particular problem that had harassed him and the rest of his team for days. He was still tinkering with it, bleary-eyed, when Murthy tapped him on the shoulder.

"That solution of yours," said Murthy. "Brilliant."

Thanks, said Swamy. I thought so myself.

"You realize, don't you," Murthy said, "that it is something that could potentially work for other businesses as well."

Swamy didn't quite get it, until Murthy spelled it out for him: "I mean, fucker, that this is something worth setting up your own company for."

The conversation stayed with Swamy, burning through his mind, and characteristically, he moved quickly. It was his idea, but it was Murthy, displaying again the financial acumen that he had previously exhibited in ordering their personal finances, who organized the money. The company they worked for gave them its blessings and some money in exchange for some equity, and venture capitalists provided the rest of the funding. Swamy took charge of product development and marketing, and Murthy kept a tight control on finances, saying yes to things that would improve productivity, and no to almost everything else.

When the time came to draw up the shareholding of the new company, Swamy had no hesitation.

Murthy suggested that the promoters' equity be divided 70–30, with Swamy taking the majority.

Your product idea, said Murthy.

"Your business idea," said Swamy. "We're splitting it straight down the middle."

Equity, it was, one-by-two.

Such careful planning, and, of course, it was the unplanned that happened. They found themselves back in India.

For several years in America, they had controlled their overwhelming homesickness; battening it down, beating it down, tying it into knots and leaving it unexpressed, except occasionally, when eating Indian food, or meeting with fellow Indian expats and talking about Indian politics and movies, or attending a sitar concert, or, best of all, on that rare greedy holiday home. There was simply no other choice but to live and work in America—until, suddenly, it appeared, there was.

The Indian economy had been changing while they were away, and Bangalore, of all places, *home,* had suddenly emerged as a significant location for software development, with software engineers to be had on the cheap. India, where, it was rumored, the streets were newly lined with venture capitalists and luscious golden-skinned damsels, trained in the coital arts of the *Kama Sutra*. Swamy and Murthy made several wary, disbelieving trips, assessing the viability of shifting their production center ten thousand miles to the east.

"It will cut costs," Murthy said finally.

"Fuck," Swamy said, for once rendered speechless by the notion of such a prodigal return.

They came home. Their parents greeted them with tears of happiness and countless marriage proposals. They met up with old friends like Ramu, and made new ones. Swamy continued traveling to America, but this time on his own terms, first class all the way, under the banner of the company he had founded, to meet with customers, to secure orders, before returning home to India to process them, and to socialize with people like Rahul, who, a few years earlier, wouldn't have given him the time of day.

Karl, Rahul's friend, now repeats, Shit, I wish I were in your place.

Swamy says nothing. Instead he sips his beer and waits for this Karl to move away, shouting at him in his mind like the commander of a Hollywood action-movie SWAT team: go! go! go! go! go!

They had met earlier that evening at the party. "Hi, I'm Karl," he'd said, and Swamy had taken him in instant aversion. He knew him. Knew him and his type. He was part of that mystical Indian tribe that, immediately upon landing on American shores, goes completely native, emerging later with Hihowyadoin accents and names like Kamalesh shortened to names like Karl.

It was one of those parties where half the people present had worked or studied in America, and were never able to let that part of their lives go, even while they returned to India to reclaim their past and plot their future. Already, the two other individuals talking to Swamy welcomed Karl in, creating a space for him, and unconsciously increasing the American intonations in their speech. Swamy found himself changing too, but in the other direction; he rapidly indianized his own accent, discarding the drawl and inserting melody, hardening his consonants so that words like "thing" sounded sharply at both beginning and end.

Karl had been in India for a few months, and was not happy. "Man," he said. "I'm surprised anyone can stick it out here."

"Oh, it works out," someone said vaguely, but with a smile that was understanding, complicit.

"Except when the power fails."

"Yeah, really. And you go shopping and you can't find shit."

"Or the phones cross-connect."

"Or when someone tells you they're gonna do something immediately, and three months later, you're still phoning. . . ."

A part of Swamy could identify deeply with everything they said; it hadn't been easy, this homecoming; India, providing opportunity and hassle in equal measure. Yet he was also keenly aware of the Great Absurdity inherent in conversations like this: the land of dreams always reconfiguring itself into the one left behind, tinged with regret and wistful desire.

Now Karl wants to know: So, are you going to be based in California again?

Yes, says Swamy, disappointment washing through his mouth at those words.

When you get settled, says Rahul, I'll come visit. We can go to Las Vegas together, I tell you, man, what chicks.

Great, says Swamy. I look forward to it.

Yeah, it is a good thing you're going, yaar. I tell you, this country is going to the dogs.

The future was not supposed to lie so.

A few months before their scheduled IPO, when all their hard work and happy clients and good publicity were set to translate into actual gain, in New York, in Bombay, where their share certificates would ascend to a value far greater than the paper they were writ upon, transmogrifying (like magic) into money in the firm and money in the bank—that was when it happened. A worldwide recession appeared, like magic, dreamed up by a drunken genie out of a bottle, cross-eyed with a hangover. It is amazing how quickly venture capital can dry up. How quickly the behemoth companies they were supplying can slide into financial constraint, how quickly they can change their orders, So sorry, yes, it's tough for us too, recession and all, seven thousand people laid off, good-bye. Kings today, interred tomorrow. As Hurree Jamset Ram Singh, Nabob of Bhanipur, might say: the interredfulness of the king in its very completeness is terrific.

Or as Murthy might say: fuck, da.

Night after disappointing night, Swamy and Murthy stayed at their desks, speaking to potential customers and financiers in countries ten thousand miles away, holding the company aloft through desire and desperation alone. Finally, after months of worry and despair—the first flush of relief. Swamy bounced into the office after spending a week in America followed by an entire weekend on the telephone. It wasn't what they'd dreamed of, it wasn't even close, but it was some sort of vindication.

"I've found a buyer," he told Murthy. A multinational firm that was willing to buy their company from them for a decent price and a job in senior management in their own company. Murthy and he could move back to America, to California, in a matter of weeks. They would still have some control over their software product, but as part of the larger organization.

It's time to go back, he said to Murthy. Things will improve, and then maybe we can try again. Just bad timing, this. It was a good idea. But now it's time to go back.

Murthy listened, as he always did, thoughtfully, quietly.

Great, he said. I think selling the company is a wise choice; we may not get another chance like this. Not so soon, anyway.

And then he said: But I don't think I will be going back to California. Bound to be something else I can do around here.

"Right," Swamy had said eventually.

"What," he'd asked, a couple of days later.

"There are good opportunities in BPO," said Murthy. "Worth looking at, at least until the climate improves for software development."

And Swamy had stared at him, caught unawares by his own surprise.

It wasn't that Murthy was wrong in his assessment: indeed, companies all over the world were busily shifting their back-office operations and customer-care call centers to India, for BPO, or "business process outsourcing," to take advantage of the relatively cheap intellectual labor available here.

It wasn't even that Murthy was choosing to think, as Swamy twitted him, like a buck-making businessman and not an idealistic software engineer captured by the dream of creating a product that would change the world.

No. Murthy might well be making the right choice. All the faith that Swamy has reposed in Murthy's judgment over the years tells him that. Swamy's surprise is directed at himself—and the sudden realization that, unlike Murthy, he does not seem to have it in himself, in this crucial moment of decision, to make that final commitment to India.

He had felt the first inklings of this a little earlier, fueled by the fear that first erupted during those long nights when things looked like they might fail, utterly and completely; when none of the arguments that he used to convince himself to return home—the opportunities, his aging parents, the wonder of being home—gave him comfort. A fear that, by staying behind now, when the going has gone so badly wrong, the fruits of all his years of hard work and sacrifice in America would never again be his for the plucking—that he would, in some atavistic fashion, revert to the state of his boyhood, stuck in India, full of longing, with America hung full and ripe and out of his reach.

In high school, Swamy and Murthy's whole world had revolved around gaining admission to the engineering college of their choice in India. The entrance exam had taken four years of preparation; they had competed with a hundred thousand others; their chances of being two of the two thousand finally selected were slim. They had studied together, but as they waited for their results, an odd constraint had developed between them. What if they were not admitted? What if only one of them was?

But such possibilities remained outside their realm. Admitted they both were, and survived together on an odd combination of brilliant peers, awful food, and meager academic facilities; repeating that feat, again and again, in different environments in a different country; a strange, undefined, never-discussed partnership of twenty years.

Murthy is laughing at something Ashwini is saying. He looks wonderfully peaceful, and for one quick minute, Swamy is again seized with doubts as to the wisdom of his own decision, doubts he is quick to dismiss as they arise.

Out of the corner of his eye, he sees Rahul wandering back in his direction. In desperation, Swamy interrupts Murthy.

"Did you bring your guitar?" he asks. "Where is it, in the car?"

Ashwini says: "I'll get it."

Murthy takes the guitar and settles it comfortably on his leg and against his body, one arm draped over it. His fingers pluck and dance their way over the strings, the other hand forming chords in leprous imitation of a dancer's *mudras*. A random run of notes and chords emerges, segueing from one barely recognized progression to another. Someone lights the second joint and it circulates, eventually reaching Swamy, who accepts it with pleasure, not removing his gaze from Murthy and the magic he is creating. And as he has a thousand times through their years together, he calls out his request.

"California Dreamin'," he says.

All the leaves are brown / And the sky is gray . . .
Soon, in perfect pitch and right on time, Ramu's voice joins

in, an Art Garfunkel to Murthy's Paul Simon. Ramu has a mild tenor voice, trained by years on the school choir and, subsequently, by singing harmonies on college bands.

The others listening join in as well, usually at the chorus, as the music takes them back a decade or more, to a thousand such song sessions around a thousand guitars on college campuses scattered around India. The music was always the same, seventies rock and roll, unchanging through the decades.

You who are on the road
Must have a code that you can live by
And so become yourself
Because the past is just a good-bye

Murthy wanders through CSNY, the Eagles, Jethro Tull, *Jesus Christ Superstar,* smiling as Swamy peremptorily tugs him from one song to another. *A long, long time ago, I can still remember, how that music used to make me smile . . .*

It has been years since Swamy has heard Ramu and Murthy sing together, and now they harmonize tentatively, slowly gaining confidence as they go, singing bye-bye miss american pie, smiling ruefully as they make an occasional mistake, mouthing the songs that have countless memories stamped into each. Memories of copying words down painstakingly from LP records and cassettes, and rehearsing, rehearsing for all those intercollege cultural festivals, trying as best they could to reproduce the ragged, magical, astonishing sounds of Neil (Young), Don (McLean), Ian (Anderson), and Roger (Waters). Old legends still abounded: how one lead singer of some college band had actually written to Ian Gillian of Deep Purple, to ask him how a voice trained in the liquid melody of *ghazals* could achieve the power it needed to do justice to a song like smoke-on-the-water, and by return mail, they said, the advice arrived—go to a field at night, it said, and scream. Scream your desire up to the sky and the power will come.

The harmonies, the smoke, wash through him, relaxing his body, opening his mind to random thoughts and impressions. He watches the moonlight strengthen, heightening the contrasts of the night, sending the sand waves scattering helplessly across the clearing towards the sanctuary of the dark shadows beyond. The music drifts to Simon and Garfunkel. *And here's to you, Mrs. Robinson. Jesus loves you more than you will know.*

Swamy feels his breath warm his lungs and heat the tips of his fingers, which press against his cheek.

" 'Gerry Niewood,' " he says, " 'on saxophone.' "

The 1981 *Concert in Central Park* is one of his favorite recordings, and Swamy is familiar with every nuance. The spoken interludes addressed to the crowd of thousands by Simon and Garfunkel between songs trickle through the cracks in the music to resonate in his mind, over and over, sometimes escaping in a carefully intoned murmur through his mouth. " 'What*anight* . . . I thought it might be . . . uh, somewhat crowded, but we seemed to have *filled*theplace.' "

There are periods in his life when he becomes obsessed with a particular piece of music, playing the same tape or CD obsessively over and over until his blood moves in rhythm and the words stamp themselves deep into his consciousness, to emerge suddenly, to sprout life at the least propitious moments. What, da? What did you say?

Swamy, people say, has a magic touch. The not-insignificant

money he has made from the sale of his company. The job that now awaits him. In these recessionary times, this is a sign of success, but to Swamy it feels strangely like indelible compromise.

He leaves tonight.

Like the nabob in the storybook, another foolish Indian abroad.

The fire is still burning strongly, kept alive by one of the little ragamuffin boys, who adds firewood to it every now and then. Murthy's glasses glint in the light; he had attempted replacing them with contact lenses at one stage, but they gave his face a raw, nude look, and finally it had all been too much to bother with the daily rinsing and cleaning routine. Now that he thinks of it, Swamy sees that there are differences in Murthy's appearance. When they had first left India for America, college life and awful canteen food had elongated Murthy, stretching him out to an incredible length but keeping him painfully thin, a constant target for his mother's concern. Stylish he had never been, with hair that flopped over his forehead onto his glasses despite applications of Brylcreem to keep it in place, and a valiant growth of fuzz over his lips and on his chin. He had dressed, whatever the occasion, in faded T-shirt, jeans, and rubber bathroom *chappals*. That was Murthy then. Now he has filled out, his clothes, though casual, are expensive and branded. Working in corporate America has taught him to style his hair without the use of pomade. Swamy recognizes these changes in himself as well. They are turning into their fathers, though a little less homespun, and with confidently deeper pockets.

Murthy places his guitar to one side, lights another joint, and inhales. The music swells from the innards of the car parked next to them, and Swamy recognizes the familiar comfort of Dave Brubeck. He glances at his watch.

He has just enough time to drive home, to collect his bags and his parents, who insist on coming with him to the airport, where he is scheduled to catch the middle-of-the-night Lufthansa flight to Frankfurt. From there another plane will fly him over the cold wastes of the Arctic, straight to San Francisco. Two flights, two days of travel. Swamy stands up and stretches. He can see people turning towards him, smiles of good-bye pinned tentatively to their faces. He does not look at them.

See you later, he says.

Murthy nods and says, Okay, then.

ACKNOWLEDGMENTS

Nikhil Kumar, for convincing me that I should; for supporting me while I did; and for enduring cheerfully the dread consequences of such rashness: having just-printed manuscripts shoved anxiously into his face in the middle of the night for that important first opinion.

Lane Zachary, agent extraordinaire, for taking this book to places never imagined, and for bolstering the journey with editorial wisdom, and, towards the end, occasional glasses of whiskey.

Susan Kamil, for her inspiring energy, intelligence, humor, and tireless commitment to bringing out the best in the book. Laughter in the longest transcontinental phone calls.

Laxam Sankaran, for providing a patient, erudite reference point on matters of Sanskrit and Tamil and cultural heritage.

Early readers Andrew, Chandran, Dermot, Kamal, Pam, Shivram, Sylvia, Vivek, and Wendy, for invaluable feedback and insights. Esmond Harmsworth at ZSH. The wonderful Fine

Arts Work Center in Provincetown, for the space to learn and explore.

C. Michael Curtis, for his encouragement and the gift of stern editorial rectitude.

For bringing the cover to life: Tania, Anandi, and Ruchika Venky at the lovely Tamarind Tree. And, of course, Asha and Shreya.

Dinesh and Jayashree Kumar, for vital structural and family support in Bangalore.

For lifesaving skills deployed daily: Abdul Mujahid, Asha Rani, Teresa Peter, and T. G. Ranganath.

Aarya, little one, source of unending joy.

The city of Bangalore; errant muse, you.

Thank you.

ABOUT THE AUTHOR

Lavanya Sankaran is a graduate of Bryn Mawr College. She resides in Bangalore, the city of her birth, along with her husband and her daughter. Her previous employments have included investment banking in New York and consulting in India. Her writing has been published in the *Atlantic Monthly* and the *Wall Street Journal*. *The Red Carpet* is her first book.